SUNDANCE: LOS OLVIDADOS

Down in Old Mexico for a hunting expedition, Jim Sundance ran into an old friend, down-and-out lawyer Jorge Calderon, who was engaged in a lonely battle to save a poor Indian tribe from slavery. The halfbreed gunfighter joined the fight against a bloodthirsty Mexican army colonel and ruthless landowner Lucas Bannerman, the mind behind the slave ring. Sundance knew how desperate and dangerous it was to try to fight the enemies of his people.

Books by Peter McCurtin
in the Linford Western Library:

SUNDANCE: IRON MEN
SUNDANCE: HANGMAN'S KNOT
SUNDANCE: LOS OLVIDADOS

PETER McCURTIN

SUNDANCE: LOS OLVIDADOS

Complete and Unabridged

LINFORD
Leicester

First Linford Edition
published October 1989

British Library CIP Data

McCurtin, Peter
Sundance: Los Olvidados.—Large print ed.—
Linford western library
I. Title
813'.54[F]

ISBN 0-7089-6763-9

Published by
F. A. Thorpe (Publishing) Ltd.
Anstey, Leicestershire
Set by Rowland Phototypesetting Ltd.
Bury St. Edmunds, Suffolk
Printed and bound in Great Britain by
T. J. Press (Padstow) Ltd., Padstow, Cornwall

1

SUNDANCE had taken out the big Remington Rolling-block .50 rifle from its wool-lined scabbard. He was cleaning it when the sergeant from the Mexican Army post arrived with the telegraph message from General Crook. For a week he had been waiting for his old friend to arrive in Las Piedras.

The sergeant handed the message to Sundance and saluted. He looked curiously from the heavy hunting rifle to the tall halfbreed with the copper-colored skin and shoulder-length yellow hair. He waited while Sundance read:

HAVE TO DELAY HUNTING TRIP. SENATOR PHIPPS AND PARTY HERE ON INSPECTION TOUR. WILL TELEGRAPH WHEN I CAN TRAVEL TO SONORA. SEND WORD IF YOU HAVE TO LEAVE. GEORGE CROOK. FORT DOUGLAS, ARIZONA TERRITORY.

1

"You wish to reply?" The Mexican sergeant spoke in heavily-accented English.

Sundance nodded. He took the pad and pencil and printed: WILL WAIT. The sergeant saluted again and went out, full of self-importance. He was impressed with his role as the bearer of a message to George Crook, the famous American general, who was as well known in northern Mexico as he was in the United States. Only a year before Crook had led a joint force of American and Mexican cavalry against Geronimo's mountain stronghold. In a short, bloody campaign he had defeated the fierce Apache raider and forced him to lead his warriors back to the reservation. Sundance had been with him then, as chief scout. At that time the two old friends had promised themselves that they would return to Mexico at the first opportunity to hunt the great cat, *el tigre*, in the wilderness of the Sierra Madre. The two men, whose friendship was a mystery to many, had looked forward to this hunt for a long time. It would be good to get away from civilization for a few weeks, to push far back into the uncharted mountains, to places where few men had ever been, sleeping in the open, cooking meat they shot, getting the stink of towns out of their lungs.

Sundance continued to work on the big rifle. Outside the *casa de huespedes* the fierce July sun beat down on the deserted street. Down the hall the room reserved for George Crook stood empty. It wasn't much of a room and Las Piedras wasn't much of a town. On one side was the desert, on the other the great threatening mass of the Sierra Madre. An ancient, crumbling cathedral dominated the town square. A mile or so outside of town was the fort. Now, with the window open, a hot wind stirring the yellowed curtains, he could hear bugles and the rattle of drums. At night the soldiers who had money came into town to drink in the cantinas, and there was much shouting and singing until they straggled back to the fort.

Sundance inspected the Remington for dust. A professional fighting man took care of his horse and his weapons before he looked to his own needs. The Remington Rolling-block was a weapon he prized greatly, for it was a gift from George Crook. Crook was known to the Indians as Three Stars, a name that Sundance himself used. The rifle was one of the most accurate in existence, a beautifully made single shot that fired a cartridge with 70 grains of black powder. It could reach out and drop a grizzly at more than 300 yards. If a hunter knew what he was doing one bullet was all he needed. A man hit by a bullet from the Remington never survived— it knocked him over like the hand of God.

The rolling block consisted of a mechanism at the breech end of the barrel which rotated about a heavy pin driven at right angles through the receiver of the rifle. To load, you thumbed back the hammer to full cock, rolled the breech-block back, exposing the breech. A bullet could now be inserted in the chamber and the breechblock flipped forward into place. It was a powerful, durable weapon —one that would last the lifetime of a man and beyond.

After Sundance finished working on the big rifle he replaced it in the water-proof scabbard and buckled the strap over the butt. Then he went out to the hallway and called the youngest son of the hotelkeeper. The boy came running, eager to earn the silver dollar Sundance always gave him to watch his weapons when he went out. This was Mexico where guns were more precious than gold, more sought after than tequila or food, a land where men would kill to gain possession of a rusty muzzle-loader.

The boy's name was Anselmo. He had dark, intelligent eyes and an excitable way of talking. "I will guard your fine weapons with my life, Señor Sundance," he said. "I will cut out the heart of the man who tries to take them." He displayed a murderous-looking knife with a ten-inch blade. He sat on the rickety chair by the window and held the knife across his knee.

Sundance smiled at the boy. "No need for any of that," he said. "I'm not going far. I'll be right next door at the cantina." He flipped the silver dollar to the boy who caught it with his left hand.

"Gracias, Señor Sundance," the boy said, smiling broadly. "I hope you stay here for a long time. I would guard your weapons even if you did not give me money. It is an honor."

Sundance wanted nothing more than to be gone from Las Piedras with its dusty streets and its swaggering, drunken soldiers, but he didn't want to hurt the boy's feelings. "It is an honor to have you as my sentry," he said as he went out into the sunblasted street.

The cantina beside the hotel was the best in town. It was called the Esplendor. The proprietor had lived in El Paso and prided himself on the cleanliness of his establishment. He called himself Joe and his Mexican-born Mormon wife did the cleaning while he drank steadily throughout the day. He wore a black suit, a white rubber collar and a yellow ribbon tie. He always welcomed Sundance as a fellow American far from home.

"Ah, my good friend," he told Sundance when he came in. "I was beginning to think you had deserted me for some other cantina. The thought of such a thing made my heart sad, but then I thought to myself Señor Sundance would never do that. Where else in all this miserable town would he find such comfort, such good food— such *cleanliness*—as in the Esplendor. Was I wrong in thinking that, my friend?"

"You speak the truth," Sundance answered formally. He knew what was expected of him. Mexicans were always formal—even when they were preparing to cut your throat. It was a country where even murderers had good manners. "I was thinking of a steak and a pot of coffee. Is that possible so early in the day?"

Joe drew himself up to his full height of five fat feet. "For no one else but you, my friend. For you I would slaughter a cow and grind coffee with my own hands. These hands!"

"Thank you," Sundance said. He sat down.

It was a good steak. He was halfway through it when the batwing doors banged open and Jorge Calderon came in. He was five years older now, but that wasn't why Sundance didn't recognize him at once. The years hadn't treated him well. It showed in the pallor of his face, the stoop in his shoulders and the shabbiness of his town suit. A brown pint bottle stuck out of one of his side pockets. He walked past Sundance to the bar and slapped it with his hand. Joe came out of the kitchen and frowned when he saw who was demanding to have his bottle filled with mescal.

"I am sorry, Señor Calderon," he began. His manner was a mixture of hostility and embarrassment. "It is better you go some place else. I have told you."

"What's the matter?" Calderon asked. He rapped the top of the bar with the empty bottle. "Don't you think I can pay for it? Or have you had your orders like the rest of them, these old women who call themselves men?"

Joe said, "I refuse to be insulted, Señor Calderon. You have been drinking. You will go away now—and stay away. No mescal for you—nothing I have to sell can be bought by you. No one gives me orders. This is my cantina and I do not want you here."

Calderon said something Sundance didn't understand and turned away from the bar, putting the bottle into his pocket at the same time. His face was angry, but his eyes had a defeated look.

Sundance called out, "Jorge, don't you know your old friend?"

It was early in the day and the cantina was empty except for the three men. In the kitchen, Joe's wife was singing in German. Calderon turned slowly to look at

Sundance. *"Dios!"* he said, "it is you! It's so dark in here I didn't see . . ."

Sundance pointed to a chair and smiled. "There's plenty of coffee, but you're not looking for coffee."

Calderon sat down heavily after they shook hands. Behind the bar Joe looked like a man who had been handed a big surprise. For want of something to do, he began to rub the bar with a rag soaked in furniture wax. It was already very shiny, but he kept on rubbing, his fat face wrinkled with unanswered questions. Though he was the proud owner of the cleanest, most prosperous cantina in Las Piedras, he didn't look happy.

Sundance, who hadn't been told anything yet, wondered what in hell was going on. "I take it you have a thirst for mescal," he said to Calderon.

"You take it right," Calderon said in English. "The hair of the dog. I had what they call a late night. Now I know what I'm doing in Las Piedras—I have the misfortune of living in this flea-

10

bitten metropolis—but why are you here?"

"In a minute, Jorge." Sundance called out, "Mescal for my friend here and fill his bottle, too."

The fat cantina owner hesitated as though he wanted to say something important. Then he shrugged and reached for the five-gallon jug of mescal behind the bar. He filled a glass with the fiery brandy and brought it to the table. Jorge Calderon gave him the empty pint bottle and he took it away.

"Nothing for me," Sundance said. "You know I can't handle booze of any kind."

Gulping down half the glass of mescal, Jorge said, "Nor can I, if the truth be told. But it keeps me going. Gets me to sleep, and keeps me asleep when I need it. Helps me forget the things I want to forget."

Sundance didn't say anything. An explanation would come in good time, or not at all. Jorge Calderon was a friend,

11

but you didn't poke around in a man's private affairs unless you were invited.

Joe came back with the bottle and set it down without a word. Then he went into the kitchen and Sundance heard him whispering to his wife. The singing started again, louder this time, and Joe came back and stood behind the bar, pretending to be busy, but trying to hear every word they said.

Jorge finished the mescal and seemed to breathe more easily. "I'll never live to be ninety if I keep on drinking that stuff," he said. "You still like to smoke *potaguaya?*"

"Now and then. Marijuana suits me better than mescal or any other booze you can name. Booze never got me into anything but trouble."

Calderon laughed. "Remember the time you broke up the bar in that fancy French hotel in Mexico City?"

Sundance remembered but didn't laugh about it. That was when they were both fighting for Juarez. Maximilian was dead, stood up against an adobe wall and shot with the rest of his generals. The long war was over and Mexico City went wild along with the rest of the country. Sundance went wild too, drinking fine French brandy straight from the bottle. He was so wild that Jorge Calderon and five men had to tie him up. Over the years there had been other wild drinking bouts until he had finally and painfully learned to leave alcohol alone.

"You still haven't said what you're doing in Sonora," Jorge said. "Don't tell me if you don't want to."

Sundance pushed his plate away, drank his coffee and told Jorge about the hunting trip with Crook. "If he can get away that's what we plan to do," he said.

"*Dios!* Now there is a man, General Crook. If only we had such a general in Sonora."

"To do what, Jorge?"

Jorge lowered his voice after glancing at Joe who was still listening behind the bar. "Your friend the general would do to the slave traders what he did to the gunrunners and renegades in your own country. He would hang them and then he would read his Bible over their graves. A just man, a religious man, your General Crook."

Sundance wondered how much mescal Jorge had been drinking. "What are you talking about? What slave traders? I thought all that was finished years ago."

"And so it was, for a while. But as long as there is money to be made out of human misery, evil men will be there to make it. The slavers are back, not as brazen as they were, but they are back. And *Dios* help me—a dying man and a drunk—I am trying to stop them." Jorge laughed bitterly. "And I am a third thing —a lawyer. Don't you think that's funny?"

Sundance said, "You often talked about it when we were with Juarez. Suppose you stop talking through that bottle and give it to me straight."

Jorge corked the bottle and put it back in his pocket. "You remember how I used

14

to say Mexico must become a country of law. Not a lot of dead laws on the books, hundreds of useless laws—but real law. Law for the poor as well as the powerful. So after the army broke up, you went back to the United States. I worked, I studied and sometimes I starved until finally, one day, I was a lawyer. Oh yes, old friend, I had big dreams then. I was going to right all the wrongs. There would be justice as well as law. I went back to Morelos—hot, damp, steamy, beautiful Morelos—and I tried. *Dios* knows how I tried! But nothing had changed, nothing was about to change because of me. The people were free— free to starve—while the landowners grew fatter than before. I worked day and night until I made myself sick. My lungs were no longer any good. But I kept working until one day a doctor told me that I would die if I did not go to the deserts of the north. So I came to Sonora."

Sundance nodded. "Get on with it, Jorge."

"The doctor said I must rest, sit in the

sunshine, breathe the dry desert air. There would still be a chance for me if I took his advice. There was some money from the sale of my dead father's fine horses. I tried to sit in the sun. I got sick of sitting in the sun. And then I began to hear things. Las Piedras is a small place after all. They were enslaving the Indians again, here in Mexico and up north in New Mexico and Arizona. Hopis, Pimas, Navahos, others. The peaceful Indians, the farmers and pueblo dwellers. They know better than to trouble the Apaches, but there are even some Apaches who have been made into slaves. Like you, I found this talk hard to believe, but it was true. It is still true. A young man will fetch many hundreds of dollars from the big hacienda owners and mine operators. Children are sold as house servants. Girls as young as twelve are sent to the south to work in brothels. They kill the old people or leave them to starve."

"You're sure about all this?"

"As sure as my head hurts. I have been

16

to some of the villages they have raided. I have talked to some of the Indians who have escaped. A young man, a Navaho, told me how he and forty other young men and girls were seized in southern Arizona and driven across the border like cattle. Your army or the Mexican army could stop it, but high-ranking officers on both sides of the border have been bribed. I have written to the Governor of Sonora, even President Diaz himself. Nothing. I have gone to court to try to force the military commander here to take action. Nothing. The law is clear and the law is ignored. Everyone here has been bought off or scared off. You can see why I am not popular."

"You have been warned?"

"Oh, yes, I have been warned. I am to leave Las Piedras or be killed. Today is the date of departure."

"Your date or theirs?"

"What do you think?"

"Are you going to leave?"

"I don't think so. I am going to die anyway so it might as well be here. I'd

17

like to live as long as I can, yet I must stay. All last night I sat in my miserable office drinking mescal, surrounded by my dusty law books. I tried to drink enough so I would have the courage to be afraid. Can you understand?"

"In a way. But you're not dead yet, Jorge."

Jorge said quickly, "I don't want you to get mixed up in this, old comrade. This is not your fight, not your country. Stay away from me and go hunting with your general when he comes. There is no way the slavers can be stopped. I see that now."

Jorge Calderon uncorked the bottle again and drank deeply from it. The singing in the kitchen had stopped and Joe looked uneasy. The big old railroad clock on the wall said it was five minutes to eleven. Outside a mongrel ran yelping down the street, pursued by a gang of children throwing rocks. Dust blew under the batwing doors, carried by the hot wind.

Jorge Calderon finished the mescal and

put the empty bottle on the table. It was a very final gesture, but not done for show. "Go with God," Jorge said as he stood up.

"God will have to wait," Sundance said quietly as two pistoleros came in.

2

THEY walked into the Esplendor like two men who owned the world. Joe dropped his bar rag and scurried into the kitchen as soon as he saw them. The back door banged as he made for the safety of the alley. Both were dressed like Mexican gunmen. But one was an American, a young, towheaded kid with nickeled Colts in a twin gun rig. Many an old lady had a better looking mustache than the wispy growth he was trying to raise on his upper lip. One of his pale blue eyes had a cast in it. He had wide, womanish hips that didn't go with the rest of his skinny body.

The other man was a full-blooded Mexican Indian, taller than most, with lank black hair and a broad brown face. He was chewing a sulphurhead match, grinding it between misshapen teeth. His oiled holster was tied down. The oil had soaked through the leather from the inside and shone dully in the dim light of the cantina. The smell of oil and sweat came from him even at a distance.

The American did the talking in a slow, easy Texas voice. He jerked his chin toward the door, but kept his hands still. "You," he said to Sundance, "you get up and get out."

Sundance stood up slowly, waiting for it to start. "I'm up," he said.

"You're doing fine," the kid sneered. "A few more steps and you'll be out the door."

"But suppose I don't want to go?"

The Mexican had been sizing up the tall halfbreed with the Bowie knife and the long barreled .44 Colt slung from his belt. He spat out the soggy match and smiled as pleasantly as he could with the ragged teeth.

"Let me esplain somethin'," he said. "You got nothin' to do with this man here. Escuse me, it ain't none a your business. We see you in town an' ask questions about you. You're waitin' to go

21

huntin' with this General Crook. We don'
want no trouble with you, all right. Our
trouble is with the lawyer."

Sundance said, "Has he been giving
you trouble?"

The Mexican smiled again. "Well, you
know."

"No, I don't know. You want to tell
me?"

"Is a long story. You don' want to get
mixed up in this."

The kid wanted to get on with the
killing; his crazy blue eyes were wide with
anticipation. A born killer, Sundance
decided—the Mexican was just earning
his pay.

"We're wasting time," the kid said.
"You get one more chance to walk out,
halfbreed."

"Listen, Jim," Jorge Calderon started
to say.

Sundance told him to shut up. "This is
between me and these two men."

The Mexican smiled and his hand
streaked for his gun. The kid was a shade
slower but still fast enough. The long-

barreled Colt was already in Sundance's hand as the Mexican's gun came out. It had just cleared leather when the first bullet ripped through his heart. The kid got both guns out together. He fired both barrels into the floor as Sundance, hardly moving the Colt, put two bullets in his chest. Now both gunmen were on the floor—the Mexican was still twitching and Sundance gave him one in the head. There was plenty of time to make it a careful shot. The heavy lead slug shattered his forehead like a hammer hitting an egg.

"Dios!" Jorge Calderon said in a hushed voice. "A blink of an eye and two men are dead. My friend, I have got you into big trouble. You better go now. Saddle your horse and ride for the border."

Sundance grinned at the soldier turned lawyer. "Everybody keeps telling me to leave, even you. You got a gun, Señor Calderon?"

The lawyer shook his head. "I do not like guns, not since we were in the war."

Sundance picked up the dead Mexican's .45 Colt and looked it over. It had a plain walnut grip and was well cared for though not new. The balance was right; everything about it was right. "You have a gun now and you better start liking it," he said, handing the weapon to Jorge. "There are times when the law needs a helping hand."

A cautious voice called from the street, "What is going on in there? This is the Chief of Police. You will stop that shooting. I warn you my men and I are armed. We are coming in now."

"That's Luis Montoya," Jorge said, putting the Colt in the waistband of his trousers. "I think he was a good man once. Now I don't know what he is. He is married and with small children."

The Chief of Police came in followed by three constables dressed in ill-fitting uniforms. Two were elderly men, the third was very young. Montoya was in his late forties, heavy without being fat, and there were large sweat stains under the armpits of his blue uniform. All four men were armed but their guns were in their holsters. Sundance hoped they remained cautious. He had no intention of sitting in a dirty Mexican jail.

The smell of gunpowder and blood was heavy in the room. The Chief gulped nervously as he looked at the bodies on the floor. The kid's eyes were open; the cockeye seemed to have straightened itself in death.

"You killed these men?" the Chief asked Sundance. "You killed Paco Mendez and Kid Ferrill?"

"If that's who they were—yes," Sundance said. "Self-defense, Chief. They came in to kill my friend, Señor Calderon. I couldn't let them do that."

"That is true, Señor Sundance," the Chief said, staring at the long-barreled Colt hanging from the halfbreed's beaded weapons belt, and at the same time trying to assert his authority. "But if these men threatened you, you should have sent for me. Now I must ask you to accompany me to the jail. Two men have been killed and I have only your word."

Jorge Calderon came out from behind the bar with a drink of mescal in his hand. "You have my word too, Montoya. You know goddamned well these two pistoleros threatened to kill me if I didn't leave Las Piedras. Why didn't you do something about it? I'll tell you something else, you fine upholder of law and order. When you heard the shooting you thought I was already dead. It was safe to come out then."

Sundance cut in before Jorge could say thing else. "Señor Calderon is understandably upset, Chief Montoya. When a man comes so close to death he says things in anger that he wouldn't say otherwise."

"Like hell," Jorge said in English, and went back to get another drink.

The Chief bowed stiffly to Sundance. "Perhaps it will not be necessary to arrest you after all, but I must warn you not to get into any more trouble while you are in Las Piedras. I can deputize all the men I need, you understand. It will not be good for you if you get into any more

26

trouble." An unexpected note of harshness crept into the Chief's voice. "After all, you are only one man. That is something to think about, is it not."

Still speaking Spanish, Sundance agreed that it certainly was something to think about.

Half an hour later, after the bodies had been carried away, they had moved Sundance's weapons and other gear to Jorge's cluttered quarters on one of the narrow streets off the plaza. This was the poorest part of the small city, and the oldest. Jorge had two small rooms on the second floor of a rundown stone and plaster building that smelled of cooking oil and hot peppers. The street itself was noisy, filled all day with Mexican Indians selling their wares. At one end of the street was a whorehouse where the girls sat in the open windows advertising what they had to offer. Only here was Jorge Calderon popular, a white, well-educated man—an *abogado*—who chose to live among the people without money or power.

Jorge lived and cooked in one room; the other was used as his office. There was a doubtful look on his face as Sundance began to put away his gear. "Are you sure you want to move in here?" he asked. "I am a rotten housekeeper, as you can see."

"As I can see," Sundance agreed. "But I've lived in worse places. I can't let them sneak up here and kill you in your sleep. I'm in this now. Don't tell me this isn't my fight or my country. My country is wherever Indians live."

Quickly he told Jorge about his long fight against the corrupt Indian ring in Washington; about how the ring stole millions of dollars from the Indians every year. "There is nothing so small that they won't steal it," he said. "The money that is supposed to feed the Indians finds its way into their pockets. The meat is usually rotten or it's horse meat instead of beef. They hold back supplies—blankets, medicine—and sell them over and over. Then they send in the soldiers when hunger and despair drives the Indians to war. Every time there is an Indian war, the ring gets a tighter hold on the money. They are our slave traders. The missionaries preach peace on earth and the cavalrymen back up the sermons with sabers."

In the sleeping room there was an iron stove with a pot of stale coffee on top of it. After it was heated to the boiling point, it wasn't too rank. Jorge accepted a cup of his own bad coffee without enthusiasm. "I don't know about this Indian ring," he said, "but I have heard talk that important men in Washington are somehow involved in the selling of Indians. A young officer who quit your army in disgust told me that."

"It figures," Sundance said. "They can't buy and sell blacks any more so the Indians are the next best thing. How does Las Piedras fit into all this?"

Jorge said, "This is where they bring the Indian captives before they are taken south to be sold. Colonel Almirante looks the other way while they are brought to

Lucas Bannerman's big hacienda five miles outside town."

"Bannerman is an American?" The name sounded familiar to Sundance. After the Civil War there was a Confederate brigadier general of that name who had narrowly missed hanging when Union troops occupied Louisiana. During the war he had taken hundreds of Union prisoners from prison camps in Louisiana and Florida and used them to work the big plantation he owned in the bayou country west of New Orleans. Many had died of disease and starvation.

"That's the same man," Jorge said. "It must be. Here in Sonora he vows to reclaim the fortune he lost when he had to flee the South. Already he has built a big house with slave labor. Your government has not been able to bring him back to stand trial because he is now a Mexican citizen. The politicians in this state, most of them, think he is a fine man who will do much for his adopted country. I know about this Bannerman because he makes little effort to keep his activities a secret.

An arrogant man, a cruel, dangerous man. I am a man of peace, but I would like to see him dead."

Sundance decided not to finish his coffee. The pot needed to be washed and scoured with rough sand. After that he would get rid of the empty mescal bottles and bean cans. "You mean you were a man of peace," he said. "If this is Lucas Bannerman from Louisiana, you won't stop him with law books and petitions. You can try, but it will finally come down to the gun. It usually does."

"What are you going to do?"

"I don't know. I think after what happened in the cantina, the next move will be up to Bannerman. He sent two of his best men to kill you, but you're still alive. Bannerman won't like that, and he'll want to do something about it. About you or about me, or both of us. How many Indians does he keep at any one time?"

Jorge rooted around in the clutter of law books and papers and dirty shirts until he found a roll of maps. He spread out a map of Sonora and weighted down the curling ends with law books. He used a broken pencil as a pointer. "This," he said, tapping the paper, "is where we are, Las Piedras. To the east the Sierra Madre, to the west the desert. There are no Indians in the mountains so he sends his raiding parties far out into the desert, beyond the desert where the Indian farmers have their villages. To the east and to the north into the United States. There are still villages beyond the desert that he hasn't raided yet. They are too far away and the trip too brutal, but that is where he must go next if he is to keep up his supply of captives."

Jorge pointed to inked markings on the map. "He has raided here and here and here, always at a greater distance from Las Piedras. The country out there is all indicated as desert, as you can see, but there are small fertile valleys where the Indians have lived in peace until now. The government is lazy and does not bother them. Even the conscripting officers for the army do not want to travel so far across such a merciless desert. But I think Bannerman, driven by greed, will send his men there. They will go there and leave nothing but sadness and desolation behind them."

"How many men does he have?" Sundance asked.

"As many as he needs," Jorge answered. "You killed two of them today. There are many more like that. They come from all over northern Mexico and the southwest. From Chihuahua, Texas, Arizona, New Mexico. The worst men in the world, drawn here by the smell of easy money. Gunmen, criminals, deserters."

Sundance studied the map. "What is that big X?" he asked.

"That is the biggest village. Bannerman's men haven't raided it yet because it is so far away. I think that is where he will strike next. By Indian standards it is a prosperous village of farmers and hunters. Of course I have never been there, but I once talked to a priest who had made his way there from the sea. It is easy to get there from the sea. What are you thinking about, my friend?"

Sundance said, "I'm thinking that somebody ought to be waiting for Bannerman's raiders when they get there."

3

"I'D like to give them a surprise they won't forget," Sundance went on. "I mean those who survive what I have in mind for them, but we can't travel all the way to the other side of that desert just in the hope that they'll raid there next. While we're there they could be raiding somewhere else. You got any way of pinning it down, Jorge?"

Jorge said, "I have an Indian working on it. He's out there now with his ear to the ground, listening to every bit of talk he can get close to. He's a good man, a tough man, but Bannerman has this well organized. I expect him back tonight or tomorrow." The lawyer shrugged. "If he gets back. Other men have tried to get information on Bannerman. They're all dead and every time they were killed it was made to look as if hostiles did it. *Dios!* The way those men died—blinded,

35

castrated, disemboweled, staked out in the sun. Where are you going?"

Sundance was standing up. "After what happened today you won't be safe," he said. "I see you have no way of locking the door."

"There is no need in this street," Jorge said. "The poor people here are my friends. Nothing will happen to me here."

"Maybe not, but a couple of dead bolts won't do any harm. Anyway, if we're going to spend any time in here we'll need more than black coffee and canned beans. You're going to be cutting down on the mescal, I hear."

Jorge grinned ruefully. "Who told you that?"

"Just a rumor, I guess. You think it's true?"

"Could be," Jorge answered.

Sundance went down to the street, but not just for bolts and supplies. A 10–gauge shotgun and a hacksaw was what he really wanted, and double–0 cartridges if they stocked them. Nothing stopped men trying to break down a door like a double blast from a scattergun. You couldn't dodge it, couldn't duck it and couldn't live after it hit you.

It was cool and dark in the street. The Mexicans lounging in doorways watched silently as he went toward the plaza on the far side of which there was a general store. A fat man with a handlebar mustache and an apron was putting up the shutters when he got there. He spoke Spanish badly and with a heavy foreign accent. Sundance guessed he was a German.

"Come back in the morning," he protested.

Sundance showed him a small wad of greenbacks and he brightened up. "You are a stranger in Las Piedras?" he said.

The answer he got was, "I'll be wanting a sack of Arbuckle's coffee, bacon, beans, canned peaches and tomatoes. You carry guns? Shotguns?"

"Everything I carry," the German said.

The last thing Sundance spent money on was a double-barreled Greener breech-loader, a 10–gauge with 32–inch barrels.

He got plenty of cartridges to go with it. The German bundled up everything and he carried the stuff back to Jorge's quarters.

When he got there Jorge wasn't looking so good. It was a cool evening and the windows were open, but his hands shook and he was sweating—that oily sweat that comes after a long drunk. He held up his trembling hands. "Here you see a champion of the poor," he said bitterly.

Sundance had been through many bouts with whiskey when he was younger and hadn't learned yet to leave it alone. "Don't start gnawing on yourself, Jorge," he said quietly. "You'll be all right. It takes time. I'll go get you some mescal and beer for your head in the morning."

Jorge clenched his hands in an effort to keep them from shaking. Sweat ran down his face as if it had been thrown there from a bucket. He wiped his face with his sleeve. "I want it, but I don't want it. I'll fight my way through this."

Sundance shook his head. "If you're too busy fighting the mescal you won't be able to fight Bannerman. I know how to get you dry." He smiled at his old friend from the revolution. "Fairly dry, anyway. I'll be back in a minute."

He had passed a cantina on his way to the plaza and he went there now. Downstairs in the dark street four Mexican Army troopers were drinking from a bottle and laughing a lot. One of them began to sing. They sounded drunk but Sundance wasn't so sure. It could be they were waiting for him. The Mexicans who were in the street earlier had all gone indoors. Sundance knew he had been right about the brave poor people of Las Piedras—they wouldn't fight for Jorge if it came to a pinch.

Sundance walked by slowly, but they didn't seen to notice him. The cantina was a few hundred feet down the street. When he got to the door he looked back and saw they were coming his way, nice and steady on their feet. There was no more singing, and they didn't even break the bottle as drunken troopers usually would. Sundance went in.

It was a small cantina, dark and smelly, and the bar was nothing but a wide plank held up by two barrels. A few Mexicans were drinking or shaking dice for drinks. The noise of the gamblers stopped and the owner went behind the bar displaying the gold teeth in the front of his mouth.

"You wish a drink?" he asked Sundance in Spanish.

"A bottle of mescal," Sundance said. "Do you sell beer?"

Behind him he heard the troopers coming in. He got ready for them.

"Oh yes, we sell beer, very good beer, Mexican beer," the cantina owner said. "How many bottles to you want?"

"Six," Sundance said, knowing that the four troopers had something to do with the killing of the two Bannerman gunmen earlier in the day. He didn't think he'd be able to walk away from this.

They didn't give him a chance to try. They came up close, two on either side of him. One of them spoke English and he pointed to the bottles the cantina owner was putting on the bar. "Hey, *Indio*," he said, "you buyin' all that good stuff there. You don' wanna be a peeg. How's about we help you drink all that good stuff there?"

"No, *soldado*," Sundance said, "that's all for me." Saying yes instead of no wouldn't have made any difference.

The trooper laughed and the others joined in. "Hey listen, *Indio*, you gonna get sick you drink all that good stuff by yourself. I think we do you a favor and drink some of that good stuff for you. Wha' you think of that?"

Sundance said, "I still think no."

"Ah, you just jokin'," the Mexican laughed, and started to reach for the bottle of mescal.

It was time to show them how it felt to be looking into the muzzle of a Colt .44, but even before his hand moved a voice spoke from the door. It was a Mexican voice, but this man's English was better. "Three guns are pointing at you. You will be dead before your hand touches your gun. You don't believe, you can look."

It was no bluff. Two military policemen

stood in the doorway with army Winchesters raised to their shoulders, pointing them at his head. The man who spoke was a military police lieutenant with a pistol in his hand. It was cocked and ready to fire.

"Now the *soldados* will take your knife and gun," the lieutenant said.

One of the military police came forward with a pair of manacles in his hand. "Hold out your hands," the lieutenant said. "Do it now."

Sundance didn't like the metallic sound of the manacles clicking open. All his life he had ranged the west and Mexico a free man, and the Indian half of him hated confinement of any kind. Even waiting for Crook in the hotel room went against his nature. Maybe he ought to choose death now while he still had a chance to die like a man. Mexican jails were as bad as any in the world. The thought of lying on a dirt floor, eating slop, waiting to be beaten, gave him a cold feeling in his head.

"What do you think you're doing?" he

asked the lieutnant, who was a young man with light skin and a bushy blond mustache that made him look more like an Englishman than a Mexican.

The lieutenant was satisfied with himself, pleased with his power. Sundance knew he wasn't doing this on his own authority. Bigger men were behind this. The lieutenant was the kind who liked to please men bigger than he was.

"What do you think I'm doing?" he sneered. "I'm placing you under arrest for menacing Mexican citizens, Mexican soldiers, with a firearm."

The trooper who spoke English now said in Spanish, "That's right, sir. When we came in we wished him a polite good evening. He became angry and called us unwashed pigs. I think he is drunk or has been drinking, sir."

He snapped to attention and saluted.

Not to be outdone, one of the other troopers joined in with, *"Estaba borracho hasta no mas."* He was as drunk as could be.

The lieutenant said there would be no

43

more talk. Sundance was going to the guardhouse at the military post. "Charges —serious charges—have been made against you," he said pompously, "and you must answer them."

As the manacles clicked around his wrists, Sundance asked, "When will that be?"

The officer puffed up his bony chest as far as he could. "That is not for me to say, nor for you to ask. You are a prisoner of the Army of the Republic of Mexico. You will be tried fairly, that I can promise you."

"I asked you when, Lieutenant."

"Get him out of here," the lieutenant ordered the two military police.

They put him in a cage wagon, one used to transport military prisoners. They took him four miles out to the fort, an old adobe structure that had probably been built fifty years before. The two guards climbed up on the seat, while the officer rode ahead on a fine Arabian. As the horses picked up speed under the brutal lashing of the driver, Sundance had to hold onto the bars to keep from being thrown back and forth. Looking out at the darkened Sonora countryside, he felt the wild rage of a captured animal.

Lights from the fort stabbed through the darkness and the challenge of a sentry rang out. The challenge was answered and the massive nail-studded wooden gates swung open. On both sides of the gate were guard towers with the sinister snouts of Gatling guns protruding from the firing apertures. It was an old fort but looked secure, and Sundance wondered if he would ever see George Crook again. There was no way to tell.

Cavalry mounts stirred restlessly as the cage wagon passed the corrals on the way to the guardhouse, a low, squat stone building with a heavy iron door and no windows. The smell of horse piss was thick in the air, and Sundance knew he would be smelling nothing else for a while. Inside the guardhouse the smells might be worse.

A private with a rifle leaned against the wall. He straightened up when he saw the lieutenant. "Guard him well," the officer said before he spurred his horse away. "If this man escapes you will spend your life in a place worse than this."

So far there had been no pushing or kicking. When the rusty door was open he was allowed to go in by himself. But they didn't take off the manacles. The door clanged shut and the key turned in the lock. It was a sound that chilled Sundance to the bone, and he cursed himself for not having killed as many of them as he could before they shot him down.

At first he stood in total darkness except for the slivers of light coming through the three air holes high in the door. He listened for the breathing of other prisoners. There was no sound. He moved cautiously around the four walls of the guardhouse, then he crossed it from one side to the other. He was alone.

Outside he heard the night sounds of the fort, the subdued voices of men and the nervous pawing of the horses. As time wore on even the horses were quiet. There was no way to tell what time it was now. All he could do was try to rely on the Indian sense of the moving earth. He sat down with his back against the stone wall, his manacled hands in front of him, and waited for morning.

In a little while he slept. A white man might have stayed awake and thought about what would happen to him when the sun came up, but Sundance, a complete professional, knew that was useless. So he slept. It was a light sleep —the sleep of a man who would be alert in a split second if danger came near, the sleep of a man whose mind knew which noises to ignore.

At dawn he awoke to the sounds of the fort stirring back to life. A bugler blew his brassy notes, a drum rolled and there was shouting on the parade ground. Doors banged as the men turned out for morning roll call. Cavalry horses neighed in the corral close to the guardhouse. To Sundance it was the same as any army post he had ever been in, except this one was Mexican and he was a prisoner.

The air holes in the iron door were set

too high to allow him to look out. He didn't try; he sat and waited. Anyway, he was still alive and not shot dead while trying to escape. That was still something to think about. If they hadn't done it last night, they might not do it at all. Of course, Colonel Almirante had given the order for his arrest, and the idea for that had come from Lucas Bannerman. He wondered if they would go through with the mockery of a military court. If they did try and convict him, what would be his punishment? The firing squad? Ten years in the silver mines to the south? Or just expulsion from the country? Sundance wished he had a drink of water.

He got it a few hours later when the door crashed open and a private came in watched by the guard outside. Without a word he shoved a tin plate of refried beans and a mug of water at Sundance. The door closed again.

Sundance sat on the floor and ate the beans as best he could with his hands manacled. The beans were cold, but there was plenty of fire in them. He drank the water slowly. He didn't finish all of it because another day might pass before he got another drink.

It was past noon when the door opened again and Sundance saw them bringing a prisoner past the corrals. The man looked like an American. He had been beaten. Blood was on his face and on his shirt. He stumbled in front of the guards. When he fell one of the Mexicans kicked him in the side. Then both guards dragged him to his feet and pushed him ahead.

The door was locked and Sundance had company. He didn't say anything, just listened to the man's heavy breathing in the almost total darkness. When the man spoke his voice was hoarse and desperate.

"Are you Sundance?" he asked. "I heard they got you too."

"Got me for what?" Sundance countered.

"For the same thing I've been doing."

"What would that be?"

"Trying to get information on Bannerman and the slavers."

"What slavers? I came down here to hunt tigers in the Sierra Madre."

The other man said in the same hoarse whisper, "You don't have to be careful with me. We're on the same side. Colonel Wingard sent me down here from San Diego. Decker is my name. I'm a first lieutenant in United States Army. You're working for General Crook, aren't you?"

Sundance let the other man talk on.

"Everybody in Las Piedras knows you're a friend of his. I think Bannerman did some checking on you the first day you showed up. Then you got that telegraph message from the general. No way to keep things secret in a town this small. What do you think they'll do to us? Don't you have anything to say?"

Sundance said, "They beat you pretty good."

"The bastards had me chained to a ring in a wall for two days. Jesus God! I hurt all over. Listen, Sundance, there's a chance we can still get out of this if we work together. Maybe we can make a break for it next time they open the door.

It's better than waiting to be beaten again . . . You still aren't saying anything."

"And you're saying too much. How do you know I'm not with them?"

"Then you know what I'm talking about?"

"I know what you're saying. You say you were sent here to track down slavers and you got caught. One more time, how do you know I'm not with them?"

"Because you're a friend of General Crook, because you're in here. The best reason—you killed two of Bannerman's top guns. You killed them before they could kill that Mexican lawyer. He was with you when it happened."

"You know everything, don't you, Decker?"

"That's my business. I've done this work before."

"But this time you got caught. How did that happen? What have you been doing since you arrived in Sonora? What were you supposed to be?"

"A mining engineer. I'm not an engineer, but my father was. I know how to talk the language. I brought along all the equipment to make it look good. As an engineer I could move around without too many questions. But I don't think it was anything I did. I think somebody in San Diego sent them word who I was. It had to be somebody close to Colonel Wingard. Not many people knew I was being sent down here. I think you were betrayed too."

Sundance said, "I thought I was in here because I killed those two Bannerman killers."

Decker didn't answer immediately. "You still don't trust me?" he said at last. "You're General Crook's friend, you must know plenty about the army. Ask me any question you want to ask. Go ahead."

"What do they call Crook in the army?"

"Old George."

"What do the Indians call him?"

"Three Stars."

"What kind of gun does he carry on a campaign?"

"A shotgun."

"What else do you know about him?"

"Plenty, just about anything you'd want to know. Before he goes into the field, he gets out his old canvas coat and plaits his beard in two places so it won't get tangled in brush. He smokes cigars morning to night and never uses dirty words. He sleeps on the ground and eats what the men eat."

"How do you know so much?"

"Damn it, you are suspicious. Because I served with him on the North Platte."

That was one of the Indian campaigns during which Sundance had not been with Crook.

"Makes sense," he said. "Just tell me one more thing and maybe we'll talk. What's the name of Crook's wife?"

Decker answered promptly, a little too promptly. "Mary Dailey," he said. He realized he had made a slip and tried to cover it. "I know her name is Mary. She's Irish—Dailey or maybe it's Haley. Something Irish like that. That all you want to know?"

"Yes," Sundance answered. "Now why

53

don't you run back to Bannerman and Colonel Almirante and tell them it didn't work. I'm down here to hunt tigers and that's all."

"What the hell's the matter with you? I told you everything you wanted to know."

"You shouldn't have told me Mrs. Crook's name. I don't know five people who could tell her name. How would a first lieutenant know it?"

Decker drew in his breath, and for a moment it was the only sound in the darkness. Then he let it out. "You lousy halfbreed savage," he said before he struggled to his feet and banged on the door of the guardhouse.

"Open up. Send for Lieutenant Novela," he said in Spanish.

Squatting on his heels against the wall, Sundance smiled to himself. After they let Decker out it was silent again except for the sounds of the fort. He drank a little of the water and waited. The day dragged on. They didn't bring him any more water, any more food. He wondered what they would try next. Maybe nothing—just a bullet. Decker's performance had been pretty good. Maybe he had been a junior officer at one time. A man like that would be useful to Lucas Bannerman. It was possible that Decker, or whatever his name was, had something to do with the crooked officers on the American side of the border.

Many hours later he woke up and heard them coming for him. It was the middle of the night.

4

"COME out, Sundance," Lieutenant Novela ordered. It was cold. The Mexican who looked like an Englishman was wearing a cape. Two military policemen were with him, both carrying rifles but not pointing them. Well, I'll know in a minute, Sundance thought with the fatalism of his Indian nature. He knew there would come a time when there would never be another sunrise for him. The way he lived, his death would be violent. It had to happen and maybe this was it. But it was good, if only for a while, to breath in clean air, to look up at the stars.

"What's it going to be?" he asked the priggish lieutenant.

Novela didn't answer. "Remove the manacles," he told one of the guards in Spanish.

Sundance rubbed his wrists and walked

where Novela was pointing. Even the moonlight was hard on his eyes after the darkness of the cell.

They crossed the parade ground, going toward a big white house set apart from the officers' quarters. Colonel Almirante was up late, Sundance thought. Lights were bright in the ground floor of the big house, and three horses were tethered out in front. When they got closer, Sundance saw they were not army stock. After posting the guards on both sides of the door, Novela told Sundance to go in.

Novela knocked and a tall, thin American who looked like a gunman opened it. Sundance went in and the lieutenant tried to follow.

"Not you," the gunman said in a soft Cajun voice. "Just Sitting Bull here." He reached out and snatched Sundance's hat from his head. "Down the hall, Geronimo, and mind your manners."

At the end of the red-tiled hallway, an archway opened into a long, low, brightly-lit room with a fire burning in a wide stone fireplace. It was a rich, comfortable room even for a Mexican Army colonel. Most of the polished tile floor was covered by a Persian carpet, and on the walls were paintings of castles and waterfalls. The furniture was dark, solid and heavy. In front of the crackling fire two men sat in deep chairs. One was a Mexican Army colonel, the other a civilian. Over the fireplace hung a large portrait of the colonel. The man who painted it had been kind to the colonel, had given him a firm chin and trimmed away much of the fat.

"Go outside and wait," the civilian told two gunmen who were standing at the other end of the room. The Cajun stayed without being told. He kept staring at Sundance as though measuring him for a coffin.

"Come here, Señor Sundance," Colonel Almirante said in perfect English. "You may sit in that chair. This is General Lucas Bannerman who has taken an interest in your case."

Bannerman said, "Please, Colonel,

don't call me 'General.' The war's over. Mister will do."

Bannerman was about fifty, but a very hard-bodied fifty. His dark hair had long streaks of white in it. He still looked like what he had been, a Louisiana planter, a man used to giving orders and having them obeyed instantly. What he didn't look like was a man who had worked Union prisoners to death for his own profit. Someone who didn't know the true story would have thought him hard but fair, a square-dealing businessman. When the Civil War broke out he had been commissioned as captain of a volunteer company. Within a few months he had risen to brigadier general. He had been very popular with his men, it was said.

Sundance sat down and waited for them to get started. Colonel Almirante talked first because, after all, he was military commandant of the province. Short and fat, resplendent in a tailored blue uniform, he tried to be more impressive than he looked by talking loudly and deliberately, as if everything he said had great meaning.

"Serious charges have been brought against you, Señor Sundance," he said. "Lieutenant Novela has already told you what they are, so there is no need to repeat them."

"Novela is a liar," Sundance said quietly.

"Lieutenant Novela is a fine young officer," Colonel Almirante said, "and he is no liar. Why talk like that and make it worse for yourself?"

"How much worse can it get, Colonel? Where's the military trial I'm supposed to get?"

"Must you persist in that tone, my friend? I'll be frank with you. You would still be in the guardhouse awaiting trial if you did not have a powerful friend. Do you understand?"

Sundance said, "You mean General Crook?"

"No one else. And I might add that Mr. Bannerman here has interceded on your behalf."

"Why would he do that?"

Now it was Bannerman's turn. "I don't know anything about these charges, but it's possible the soldiers you had the trouble with heard of your friendship with Jorge Calderon. That man, for reasons of his own, has been stirring up the Indians all over Sonora. If an Indian war breaks out, those men and others will have to fight it. Wait, let me finish. Calderon has been spreading wild stories about Indian slavery. For God's sake, man! In this day and age! And he's been spreading stories about me. I know what I stand accused of back in the States. I'm not a man who tries to justify myself, but that isn't true either."

"What is true? They say you worked Union prisoners until they dropped or died of swamp fever."

Bannerman threw his cigar in the fire with a gesture of impatience. "Damn it to hell! Everything produced on my plantation was at the disposal of the Confederate Government. It wasn't producing enough so I was ordered—yes, ordered—

to take Union prisoners from several camps. Many of them came from Andersonville and were glad to get out. I know what Wertz did at Andersonville, and they hanged him for it. Properly so, in my opinion, and I'm as loyal a Southerner as ever lived. If men died it was none of my doing. Everything was in short supply all over the Confederacy—food, clothing, doctors, medical supplies. If a man got sick he died because there was no way to treat his sickness, be it swamp fever or anything else. But we lost the war and someone had to be blamed. I was blamed. I ask you, do I look like that kind of man?"

Sundance didn't answer that. "Jorge Calderon says you're enslaving Indians. I say that because you already know it."

Bannerman said, "Calderon is a dying man with a mind rotted by mescal. Why do you believe these stories of his?"

"Because he was an honorable soldier in the revolution. I know because I fought with Juarez too."

Bannerman took out a leather case and

selected a cigar. Between the puffs of lighting it, he said, "The revolution was a long time ago. Times change, men change, men go crazy with too much liquor. Today he sees himself as another Juarez. By his own word he has declared war on the rich and powerful." Bannerman smiled. "At least I'm rich and I'm a foreigner."

Colonel Almirante protested. "Not a foreigner. You are a respected citizen of the Republic."

Bannerman smiled again. "To Jorge Calderon I'm an enslaver of poor Indians."

"Then you didn't send those two gunmen to kill him if he didn't leave Las Piedras?"

"Those men worked for me. Why try to deny it? But they acted on their own. No doubt they heard the stories he was spreading about me. All my people are loyal."

"Even the killers?" Sundance said.

"Not killers. Call them gunmen if you like. That's what they were. This is hard country here and you have to be just as hard to keep what you have. I do my own fighting, but I can't do it alone. Does that make sense to you? It should. You've been fighting and killing all your life."

Sundance decided that Lucas Bannerman was the smoothest liar he had met in his life. "Colonel Almirante says you interceded for me. Why is that?"

Bannerman had an easy answer. "Because you killed my two men and your trouble with those soldiers may have had something to do with that. I didn't want to be blamed for one more thing."

"You mean I'm free to go?"

Colonel Almirante felt it was his place to answer that. "Not yet, Señor Sundance. Two generals, both fine men and fine soldiers, have spoken up for you. But I must warn you against associating with this madman Calderon. It's not only Mr. Bannerman he has accused of this unspeakable crime. Other big ranchers and mine owners have been named by him. He will only get you into serious trouble if you continue to associate with him. Unless he stops—and I do not think he will—someone is sure to kill him. You do not want to be killed too."

Sundance knew a threat when he heard one, even when it was put in very careful English.

Bannerman didn't say anything.

Colonel Almirante went on. "Señor Sundance, take my advice and stay away from him."

Bannerman stood up rubbing his hands together. "Before you leave, Sundance, I'd like to point out one more thing. Calderon will tell you, maybe has told you, that there are Indians working on my ranch, in my mines. All true. The difference is they're there of their own free will and get paid just like any other man. I wouldn't make this offer to any other man, but your Crook's friend so I'll make it to you. Come on out and see for yourself."

"Thanks," was all Sundance said.

"You came here to go hunting with General Crook," Colonel Almirante finished. "Wait for him and enjoy your hunt. The Sierra Madre is wild and beautiful. I hope I will have the pleasure of the general's presence at dinner some night."

Crook, Sundance thought, would just as soon as eat off the same plate as a snake than eat dinner with this fat thief.

"I sincerely hope so," Colonel Almirante said. "And now your horse has been brought from town and is waiting for you outside."

On the way back to Las Piedras, Sundance checked several times to see if he was being followed. He wasn't, but he knew they would be watching him from now on. Years back in the Colorado Rockies, Three Stars—as Sundance always called the general—had saved his life by shooting down a maddened grizzly that was coming at him full tilt. Now, once again, he owed the old soldier his life. What puzzled him was how Three Stars had known he was in a Mexican jail. There was no telegraph office in Las Piedras. The fort had a telegraph line, but no one had sent a message from there. The only town of any size was seventy or eighty miles to the north. He knew that because he had passed close to it on his way south. And yet Three Stars knew where he was; he had used his fame and power to stop them from killing him.

Red was streaking the sky by the time he got back to Las Piedras. The town was still asleep except for a rooster crowing now and then. In front of a closed-up cantina a drunk lay snoring, an empty bottle in his hand. All the way back from the fort he wondered if he would find Jorge dead. The arrest and the two nights in the guardhouse could have been a plan to get him out of the way. He vowed that if they had killed Jorge, Bannerman and Almirante would die—no matter how many soldiers and gunmen they put between them and death.

He put his horse away and walked back to Jorge's quarters. When he got there he looked up at the windows. No lights. He drew his gun and went up the stairs quietly. The door was open a few inches, and there were no sounds inside. There was almost no light in the hall, so he had as much of an advantage as any killer who might be waiting inside. It didn't make sense that they would let him go just to kill him here, but you never knew what kind of twisted scheme Bannerman had worked out.

Standing to one side of the door, he kicked it open and waited. Nobody shot at him. He went in fast and waited again, standing in the semidarkness with the Colt cocked in his hand. Then he reached into his pocket and found a sulphurhead match and struck it on the wall. The light that flared showed nothing but the clutter of his friend's rooms. He lit the lamp on Jorge's desk and carried it into the next room. Empty like the other one. No blood anywhere, no sign of a struggle. He bolted the door and sat down to think. He had to face the cold fact that Jorge could long be dead, buried far out in the hills, or stripped and left for the buzzards. The buzzards would leave nothing but a skeleton in a single day. He would wait for a while and then search for his friend. But how long would he wait and where would he look?

An hour had passed when someone tried to open the door. There had been no footsteps on the stairs. Now the door handle was being moved. Then a voice called out, "Jorge, are you in there?" The question was repeated, louder this time.

Moving silently on moccasined feet, Sundance drew his gun and shifted it to his left hand. Now! He pulled the bolt back and the door open at the same time. He found himself looking at one of the biggest men he had ever seen, an Indian taller and heavier than he was. Their eyes met and locked for an instant, then the Indian's huge hand shot out and trapped his left hand in an iron grip. He felt the Colt being torn from his hand. The Indian's huge left fist knocked him back into the room as if he had been hit by a club. His spine jolted against the edge of the desk and he went down. The Indian threw the gun away and tried to jump on him with both feet. He twisted out of the way and the floor shook under the big man's weight. He jumped to his feet while the Indian bored in after him, both fists swinging. Sundance pulled the Bowie knife from his belt and made a thrust for the Indian's belly. For all his bulk, the Indian moved as gracefully as a panther. He drew his own knife, another Bowie, and came at Sundance again. In the early morning light they fenced back and forth with the great killing knives, more like short swords than anything else. Steel clanged on steel as they tried for the soft parts of their bodies. Sundance nearly lost a hand when the Indian changed his fencing tactics and tried for a downward chop. He caught the chop on the back of his own blade. The impact sent pain vibrating all the way up to his shoulder. Then they circled in the cramped little room . . .

Suddenly Jorge Calderon was in the doorway and rushing toward them, white faced and horrified. "*Alto! Alto!* Stop!

Stop! You crazy men." The frail lawyer got between the two powerful fighting men and tried to push them apart. They separated before his trembling hands, and suddenly his terror turned to the fury that often comes with relief. He punched Sundance in the chest, then he turned and slapped the Indian in the face. Neither blow had any force and the two men, coldly trying to kill each other a moment before, began to smile.

Jorge raged on for a while, then he smiled too. "You crazy men! You fools! You *cretinos!* What were you trying to do?"

"I think we were trying to kill one another," Sundance said, still smiling.

"*Imbecil!* You are the same, Silvestra. My heart jumped in my chest when I saw what you were doing. How did this stupid and terrible thing come to happen?"

Sundance told him. "Now calm yourself, Jorge," he said. "Nobody's even nicked. Your friend here knows how to handle a knife. You were very good, Silvestra."

71

The Indian acknowledged the compliment. "And you too, Sundance," he said with grave politeness.

Jorge was ready to flare up again. "Stop this stupid talk of who is good with a knife. In a civilized world there would be no guns, no knives meant to kill other men. I think I am going to fall down. I am sick, I am tired. I have ridden seventy miles and back in two days and what do I find? The only two friends I have in the world . . ."

Jorge's voice trailed off and he slumped into a chair, gray faced with exhaustion. He lay back and closed his eyes. "*Por favor*, a drink, a big drink."

Sundance poured from the bottle of mescal. Jorge gulped it down and the glass was filled again. "I am so tired, so tired."

"What else could I do but ride to Meseta after I heard the soldiers had taken you," he said a few moments later. "And every mile I prayed you were still alive. I cursed myself for getting you mixed up in my troubles."

"Go easy," Sundance said. "You've got to rest, sleep. We can talk later."

"No! No! We will talk now. What did they do to you at their cursed fort?"

"Nothing," Sundance said. "They were very polite after the colonel got the telegraph message from General Crook. I think I'd be dead now if it hadn't been for you."

Jorge said wearily, "I knew reaching the telegraph office at Meseta was the only chance. I am not a religious man, but now I am ready to give thanks to God that you are still alive. Those dogs! Those filthy animals!"

"Bannerman was there," Sundance said. "He said you have made yourself crazy with mescal. He's right. You are crazy. To ride seventy miles and back in two days!"

"It was nothing," Jorge said with fierce Mexican pride. "I still have some money. I changed horses three times."

"It was a ride of great courage," Silvestra said gravely. It was the first thing he said since the fighting stopped.

Jorge opened his eyes and looked at the Indian. "Let us stop all this foolish talk of courage. What did you find out? Did you discover where they will strike next?"

"Yes. It is as you thought," Silvestra said. "At the Pima village on the far side of the desert. A pueblo of farmers and hunters, with eighty or ninety Pimas, maybe more. They live high on the mesa and farm the valley below. The slavers will start for this place in three or four days. It will be a bigger party than before, with many guns."

"How did you discover this?" Jorge asked, now alert in spite of his fatigue. "You must be sure. It is a pitiless desert we must cross to get there."

Silvestra said with a savage smile, "I know because one of the slavers told me. I had been watching the Bannerman hacienda with the *catalejo*—the telescope —you gave me. New men I had never seen before were arriving, so I thought something big is about to happen. One night I caught one of the slavers on the road between this town and the hacienda.

Then I took him to a quiet place in the hills. At first he did not want to talk, but finally he did. In the same quiet place I buried him along with his horse. I buried everything. I hated to bury the saddle. It was a fine saddle."

"You buried a horse!" Jorge was so amazed he said it again. "You buried a horse, Silvestra?"

Sundance smiled. Looking at the huge Indian, he almost felt sorry for the dead slaver. His death had not come quickly.

"It had to be done," Silvestra answered. "Nothing could be found or they might suspect the truth. It took much digging."

"He's right," Sundance agreed. "If they even found his hat it would tell them too much."

"Of course. I am not disputing that, Sundance. You know, Silvestra, for a good Indian who was raised in a Franciscan mission you have turned out very badly."

Jorge and Sundance laughed. "So it has

been said," Silvestra said with only the trace of a smile.

Jorge unrolled his map of Sonora and tapped it with his finger. "There it is, Canon de Nutria. That's where we must go to plan your surprise. *Dios!* What country we must cross to get there, but cross it we will. Have you made a plan?"

"After you eat and sleep we'll talk about the plan," Sundance said.

"I will sleep first, then I will eat," Jorge decided, sounding very definite about it.

Sundance was just as definite. "No, Jorge, first you will eat, then you will sleep. That's the best way."

Jorge hadn't drunk very much, but the mescal added to his fatigue made him drunk. Now his black eyes blazed with anger. "Who are you to give orders to me? There are no generals in this army. You can be a general when the fighting comes. Here we are all equal."

"Not so, old friend. Just for this day I have appointed myself general of the cookstove and I say you eat before you sleep."

Jorge saw Silvestra smiling gravely and got mad again. He shook his fist at the big Indian. "What are you grinning at, you undertaker for horses?"

But, in the end, he did what he was told.

5

JORGE slept all that day and half the next night. Now he was up again and they were sitting by his desk talking about the fight to come at Canon de Nutria. They all knew it wouldn't be easy, and some of them might not come back. Jorge was drinking a bottle of beer, still irritable that Sundance had poured out the rest of the mescal. He still looked tired.

"Of course I'm up to it," he said. "I'm a Mexican and I know this desert."

Sundance shook his head. "You don't know this desert. If you can't make the trip, say so now. Silvestra and I can do this alone. We don't want to have to carry you. You're tired and you're sick. That ride to Meseta nearly killed you. Crossing that desert, the way you are, could finish you off."

Jorge didn't like beer, but it was all he

had to drink. "I'm finished anyway, so what's the difference. A few days from now or a few months. I tell you I'm all right."

Silvestra, like Sundance, didn't agree. "You are sick, Jorge, and you know you are sick. We can take you to a safe place and you can rest there until we return."

Outside it was dark and the town was quiet. They had turned the lamp down to a glimmer. They had been talking for an hour and there was still much talking to be done.

"What do you know about my sickness?" Jorge asked the Indian. "Since when did you get to be a doctor?"

Sometimes it was hard to be patient with Jorge. "He doesn't have to be a doctor," Sundance said, but before Jorge could snap back at him he added, "and you wouldn't listen anyway. All right, it's settled—you're coming along. Silvestra says the dead slaver told him twenty men or more will be in the raiding party. That's just about every gunman Bannerman has on his payroll. Not every man but almost. If we do this right—kill every last man—it will set Bannerman back a long way. You sure they've been watching this place, Silvestra?"

"You know they are, Sundance."

"Then how are we going to get out?" Jorge looked puzzled. So was Silvestra.

The question was one that Sundance had been turning over in his head all day. If they just rode out, even armed to the teeth, they wouldn't get far into the desert before Bannerman's riders caught up with them. No matter what kind of fight they put up they would still die.

"How?" Jorge repeated.

Sundance spoke to the Indian. "You want to take a chance? They know you're working with Jorge, so it won't be safe if you go out in the streets of the town by yourself. In here we're safe enough for the time being. I'm safer than either of you because of General Crook. That's also for the time being, but that will change."

The Indian's face showed nothing. "What do you want me to do, Sundance? I have come this far with Jorge."

It might work, it might not. Sundance said, "In a few hours the town will be awake and the cantinas opening up. Just about then I want you to go out of here staggering and yelling with a bottle in your hand. Then stand in the street and look up at the window and call Jorge every dirty name you can think of— coward, pig, child raper, drunkard, traitor. Yell coward and traitor many times, but use the other names too."

"I know many dirty names," the Indian said.

The lawyer's mouth hung open in astonishment and he looked from Sundance to Silvestra. "In the name of the Savior what is going on here? Dog! Pig! Coward! Traitor! Drunkard!"

Silvestra's brown face was solemn. "The last name will not be a lie."

Turning back to Sundance, Jorge said, "Would you please tell me . . ."

"You have finally turned yellow and are leaving Las Piedras. Mescal has rotted your courage away and you no longer have the stomach for the fight against the slavers. You've become a drunken coward. You're running like the mongrel you really are. You're packing up and pulling out for good. Silvestra will say all this. When he finishes shouting that in this street, he will go into the cantinas and say it. He has risked his life for you and you have betrayed him, betrayed all Indians. He will curse me too because I encouraged you in your betrayal."

"Then what?"

"Then you will leave Las Piedras, but not before Bannerman hears everything we want him to hear. A few hours should do. I'll leave after Silvestra starts acting like a drunken Indian. You'll have to stay here by yourself for a few hours. That's another chance, but I don't see any other plan that will work. Later I'll buy a horse and wagon and come back here to get you loaded up."

Sundance went on. "We'll load the law books and your legal papers in the wagon. Along with the guns. We have enough guns. They'll be wrapped in sacking so Bannerman's spies won't know what they are. We'll shake hands when it's finished and then you'll head back to Morelos a drunken, defeated man. Keep going on the south road until you're sure you're not being followed. They may not follow you at all. If they do, keep going. Don't stop till you're clear. Then take the wagon off the road and wait. Stay there for as long as it takes but stay out of sight. We'll find you and that's where it begins."

"How long do you think I'll have to wait."

"Maybe as long as a day. They may watch me, watch Silvestra for a while. I don't think so. Silvestra is just a dumb Indian and I no longer have any interest in your cause. But we must have time to get everything set."

It was less than an hour to first light.

Sundance told Silvestra he'd better drink some beer to get a smell on his breath. The big Indian nodded. He must have known what Sundance was thinking because he said, "I will not get drunk in the cantinas. All my life I have seen what tequila and other liquor has done to my people, and to other men."

Jorge scowled. "This is worse than being at a temperance lecture."

Sundance asked Silvestra if he was sure he had enough dynamite hidden away. "It isn't sweated? You know what sweated means?"

"I do," Silvestra answered. "Sweated is when the nitroglycerin begins to ooze and bead on the outside of the sticks, a thing that happens when the dynamite is old and dangerous to handle. No sweating. Yes, I have stolen enough dynamite in the past year. Stick by stick I stole it from Bannerman's mine. It was my hope that it could be used to destroy his fine hacienda, to close his mine for good. It will be good to use it against his slavers."

At last, after all the hours of talk, sunlight was slanting through the windows.

"It's time," Sundance said.

Not much more than twenty-four hours later they were heading into the Sonora desert, traveling west on a downslope. At first there were foothills falling down and away from the first slope of the Sierra Madre. Here the bare, brown hills were covered with thickets of cacti, many kinds of acacias, mesquites, paloverdes and brittle bush. In the distance was a thorn forest and beyond that black lava beds. Here and there an organ pipe cactus stood up taller than anything else. It was an hour past noon, but the fierce Mexican sun seemed to be suspended directly overhead, as if daring them to ride out into country that had claimed so many lives. Beyond the foothills the desert stretched out in front of them, bleak and hostile, shimmering in the sun. Each man carried four canteens slung on both sides of his saddle.

"Looks like we got out without being spotted," Jorge said, sweating badly though the long trip had just begun. "You made a good plan, Sundance."

Jorge had a brave heart, but he was not a professional. "Don't be too sure about anything," Sundance said. "Bannerman

85

didn't get to be where he is by chance. All we can do is keep going and see what happens. Either way we have our work cut out for us. The best we can hope for is a head start."

They skirted the thorn forest when they came to it, and that took up some valuable time. On the other side of the lava beds the country began to level off. After that there was nothing but yucca, creosote bush and cactus short grass.

An hour later they stopped to water the horses and let them rest. The sun beat down with savage force. Even in the shade of a big yucca anything metal was blistering hot to the touch. They started off again and now the desert was different, even more forbidding than it had been. The sand was softer and whiter than it had been. Now and then there were dunes that rolled away for miles. The sun's glare on the white sand was hard on their eyes.

"*Dios!* What country!" Jorge said, tying a bandanna around his forehead to keep the sweat from running into his eyes. "What pigs these slavers must be! To ride across such country just for money!"

Sundance turned to scan the country behind them. There was nothing but a *zapolote*, a turkey buzzard, wheeling lazily in the sky. "For them money is the best reason," he said. "They will fight and suffer and die for money."

"But surely they are cowards as well as greedy men?"

"No," Sundance said, "men can be brave as well as bad. There may be more brave bad men than brave good men. That is a fact you must face, Jorge. You would like to deny it, but it is true."

Jorge said irritably, "I do not like your truth, Sundance, but it is too hot to argue. *Dios!* It is so hot!"

"It will be worse tomorrow," Silvestra said quietly. "In the dead heart of the desert will be the worst part of all. Out there even the Gila monsters lie still in their burrows under rocks when the sun is overhead."

"I knew I could count on you to say

something cheerful," Jorge said. "Have you any other good news?"

"It'll be cool in an hour," Sundance said. "Everybody's going to feel better then."

Now it was close to six o'clock and the sun was beginning to weaken. They rested and watered the horses again. They kept going until the light was gone and it was time to bed down for the night. After they hobbled the horses they chewed on dried meat and took careful sips of water. Too tired to talk, Jorge rolled himself in his blankets and was instantly asleep.

Sundance said he would take the first watch. "Tonight we'll let Jorge sleep," he told Silvestra. "In the morning he will argue that we should have waked him, but he'll be glad we let him sleep."

During the night it was cold, with stars bright and frosty in the limitless sky. Sundance sat with a blanket draped over his shoulders until it was time to rouse Silvestra. There was no need; the big Indian was already awake.

"Everything's quiet," Sundance said quietly. "How is Jorge?"

Silvestra said, "He sleeps badly but he sleeps. After he sweats out the mescal he will be all right. Then his dreams will no longer be filled with demons."

Sundance rolled out of his blankets at four the next morning. A cool wind blew across the desert; a glimmer of light showed on the eastern horizon. Within hours the wind would blow furnace hot as the sun crept up to its full blazing fury, but for the moment this terrible land was still and peaceful.

Silvestra stood up and let the blanket fall from his shoulders. He shook his head. "Nothing," he said.

"Nothing all night."

Sundance watered the horses and let Jorge sleep until it was time to go. By then the sky was washed in red and the wind had grown warmer. The water in the canteens was cold and Jorge's teeth chattered as he drank from his. To head him off, Sundance said, "We let you sleep because you needed the sleep. That's all we want to hear about it."

Jorge nodded as he stoppered his canteen. "All right," he said.

They kept going all that day and the day after. The sun beat down with relentless force, trying to kill them every mile they traveled across the wasteland. Jorge had sweated the last of the alcohol from his system. Though he was pale, he was in better spirits. He didn't snap back when one of the others said something.

During the day, the three men said little. At first Jorge, a man of many ideas, was inclined to talk, but as time passed the overwhelming silence of the great desert caused him to fall into a relaxed silence of his own. Sundance began to feel better about his old friend; his quiet mood showed that he was getting a hold on his nerves.

When men who trust each other have traveled a long way together there comes a time when a gesture or a single word will do in place of many words. For Sundance, Jorge and Silvestra, a gesture was often enough. It was when the sun went down and camp was made that they talked—and their talk was seldom of the slavers and the fight that lay ahead. They knew what lay ahead, but talking about it wouldn't make it happen any faster, or tell them how it would end. Water was running low, but they didn't talk about that either.

On the third night they were camped on the edge of what had been a lake thousands of years before. It was too late to cross and so they made camp. The sun was gone, but the wind was still hot. They were chewing dried meat and taking careful sips of water, barely touching the mouths of the canteens to their lips. They hadn't made a campfire since the long journey began.

Jorge began to laugh and they looked at him. "Don't worry, I'm not going crazy. I'm going sane, I think. I was just thinking this is a hell of a way to take a cure from the mescal. Oh, I don't say I don't think of it—I'd be a liar if I said I didn't—but when I know I can't have any, I can accept that."

Jorge laughed again, took one last bird-like drink of water, and stoppered his canteen. "You wouldn't have a bottle of mescal stowed away in your saddlebags, Sundance? You too, Silvestra?"

Sundance smiled. "Not a drop, old friend. Silvestra is drier than I am."

"True," the big Indian said.

"There you are," Jorge said. "I've won my case."

"Maybe he has no mescal, but he's still crazy," Silvestra said. "Our friend, the judge, thinks he's in court."

Sundance, his strong white teeth working methodically, patiently on the tasteless jerked meat, smiled again. "Don't be too hard on the judge, Silvestra. He knows what he's saying and so do I. You say you haven't been through it, but I have. It takes a shock or something like it to shake a *barrachon* —a drunkard—loose from his bottle."

Silvestra thought about that for a while. "What was your shock, Sundance?"

"General Crook said he'd have me shot if I ever got drunk again," Sundance said. Sundance never laughed, but he could smile when he was with friends. He smiled now. "General Crook said I was no good to myself or to the world the way I was. A bullet would be a kindness to me. He was right."

The big Indian said gravely, "It is good to have such a good friend."

They ate in silence for a while. Then Silvestra said, "Is it true, Sundance, that in your country there are places where rich men go or are sent to take the cure from alcohol? A rich American I once guided into the Sierra told me that. He was drunk when he told me. He had been to such a place, he told me, but the cure had not worked. So he hired me to take him far into the mountains and to tie him up when the craving for alcohol was upon him. He paid me well and told me— dared me—to find his whiskey bottles and to break them when I found them. He had many burros loaded with much equipment and I had to work hard to find all his bottles. I had to take his guns away before I broke the bottles. He was a wild man, though kind sober. He fought like a tiger when I put the ropes on him. It was the hardest money I ever earned as a guide, but I felt proud and useful when after a week in the cold, clear air of the mountains he stopped shaking and ate heartily what I cooked for him."

"Then what happened?" Jorge asked.

Silvestra said, "At the end of ten days this rich American said he was going to be all right—and we should start back to Las Piedras. I was better than all the doctors in the United States, he swore. We were brothers for life, he declared with much sincerity, and he would name me gratefully in his will."

"For Christ's sake," Jorge said. "I just know this Indian is leading up to something. I just know he is."

Jorge sounded all right, so Sundance was able to smile. "It's his story. Let him finish. What happened, Silvestra?"

"This rich American raced me down the mountain like a goat. In all my life I had never seen a sickly man with such energy. He bounded ahead of me with such energy that I feared his heart would stop. Or that he would stumble and fall from a high place and injure or kill himself. This way we traveled—ran—for days until the mountain was behind us and Las Piedras was in sight. When it was he pulled much money from his pocket, thrust it upon me and said it was time to say goodbye."

Silvestra paused and looked at Jorge. "That night, very late, I found him reeling in the main street, very drunk."

But all Jorge said was, "No wonder he got drunk, you damned Indian. Two weeks in the mountains with you, I don't blame him."

Sundance smiled. "Good for you, Jorge. And since you're feeling so great —why don't you take the first watch?"

Getting across the dead lake was the hardest part of the journey. What had once been mud was now stone, cracked and jagged, baked to its present state by century after century of sun. There was no way to get around the lifeless inland sea unless they were prepared to lose many days of time. To the north and to the south it barred the path of the traveler. It took them three days to cross it. Nothing grew, nothing lived on its surface, not even the hardiest of desert growth. If it had been prairie, they could have crossed it in less than a day. Much less than a day.

By the time they reached the other side of the lake the water was gone. They had saved the last of it for the horses. The animals were beginning to falter and wouldn't last much longer without water, fodder and rest.

"It's not too far now," Silvestra said, "but in this country any distance is great."

That night they talked little; their thoughts were on water. They started again early in the morning and by mid-afternoon they were traveling on an upward slant. This went on for many miles. It was almost dusk before they came to a level place, and from there they could see a line of mesas that ran along the horizon about twenty miles in the distance. In the clear dry air, the mesas looked close enough to touch.

Silvestra pointed to the biggest and highest of the mesas. "To get to the foot of the mesa we have to go through Canon de Nutria. The canyon splits the cliff face and runs back for a distance. They will see us long before we get there."

There was no use going on after dark, so they camped where they were. All the way across the desert they had checked their back trail. Now they were up high enough to be able to see back for many miles. But nothing stirred out there in that great emptiness. Not even a buzzard kited in the hard blue sky. No sun glinting on metal. Nothing at all.

In the morning they were up before the sun, silently preparing their horses for the final part of the long journey. They were well on their way by the time the sun was hot. In hours they started to come up out of the desert. Not much later the mesa was dead ahead, a great escarpment of red stone that all but blotted out the sky. Then they went up a long slope with big rocks along its spine. Silvestra pointed and they led the horses through a narrow draw that would have taken a stranger a long time to find. Out of the draw, going down the far slope, they were finally in Canon de Nutria.

Fruit trees and other crops grew along the west slope of the canyon. The slope climbed by stages to the foot of the mesa. Corn and beans, melons and peach trees flourished on the slope because there was water as well as sun.

"Up there is the village," Silvestra said, pointing. "On the top, back from the rim, is the village."

Hours of sun remained and the Pima farmers should have still been working. But the slope was deserted. "They're watching us," Silvestra said. "They have been watching us for a long time."

Silvestra led them to the place where the trail to the top of the mesa began. It started from behind a jumble of rocks big as houses that had torn loose from the side of the mesa. The beginning of the path was hidden and the path itself couldn't be spotted, even by a man with binoculars. If the Pimas had been warlike people, as the Apaches were, they could have knocked the slavers or anybody else to the bottom without any trouble. But the Pimas had been farmers and hunters long before the Spanish arrived in Mexico.

Leading his horse, Silvestra went first. In one place where the path broke and fell away, they had to jump across and then coax the horses to jump. Silvestra's Indian-trained animal did it easily, but it took some doing to get the others across. Finally, they reached the top and looked back with wonder at the terrible desert they had crossed. At first there was nothing, then they all saw it at once—a stirring at the top of a sand dune many miles away.

Sundance looked at Silvestra. "How soon do you think they'll get here? They must have started out ahead of time to get here this fast."

"They won't get here tonight," Silvestra said. "Late in the morning. They look close, but they're still a long way out. What time tomorrow depends on how early they start. But I think they will be in no hurry."

The three men turned away from the desert to look at the Pima village. All its people stood there silently, waiting for them to do something.

The top of the mesa sloped back from the rim. Silvestra took the lead because he knew a little of their language. An old man with a wrinkled face and long gray hair spoke in a high-pitched voice. Silvestra translated as best he could:

"Water, meat, fruit, women if you want women."

More talk followed. Silvestra turned and said, "I have told the chief that we are tired and hungry and want his

100

permission to rest here. It's all right to go down now. Later we will explain to the chief and the village council the reason why we came."

The three men were fed stewed rabbit by the Pima women. For dessert there were peaches, but the cold, clear water was best of all after days of enduring the brackish water in their canteens.

Silvestra began to explain to the chief. No fear showed in the old man's face when he finished. Now the chief spoke and Silvestra translated.

Silvestra said, "The chief knows the slavers are raiding again as they did in the past. Bad news travels even across the desert. It makes him sad to know the slavers are coming to his peaceful village. But why do the slavers come so far to make slaves of a handful of harmless Pima farmers? I told him because the slavers can get almost any price they want for the right captive. Because, once in captivity, men and women must work like dogs until they die."

But even then the chief said the Pimas

would not fight. It had been centuries since a Pima had spilled blood. The three strangers could fight if they wished, but the Pimas would not take part in any killing, even if it meant being sold into slavery.

The chief walked with them while they looked over the abandoned part of the village, the part they saw when they first climbed to the top of the mesa. The Pimas who had lived in the abandoned stone-walled, mud-roofed houses were all dead, had been for many years.

Sundance thought this was where they would finish off the slavers. "We could keep them down below, but the fight would never finish. In the end they might just ride off and head back for Las Piedras."

Silvestra carried the dynamite and Sundance placed it, judging how the walls of the abandoned stone houses would fall when the charges were exploded with rifle bullets. He figured the slavers wouldn't bring the horses to the top; one or two men would stay with horses while the others climbed.

When they came they would get a surprise. The last surprise of their lives.

6

"IT'S a simple plan," Sundance said, after the last of the dynamite had been placed. "The men will move back to the far side of the village. A few women and children will stay on this side. It's their job to lead the slavers into the trap."

Silvestra said, "The chief thinks some of the women and children will be shot."

"They won't shoot anybody at four hundred dollars a head," Sundance said. "You know that as well as I do. Tell the chief his people will be all right. After today he won't be bothered by slavers again. But the women and children have to get out of the way fast. They're to show themselves, then run. They can't be too close to the dynamite when it starts to go."

In a few minutes Silvestra came back

and said it had all been explained to the chief.

Sundance had been thinking. "If they rode all night they could be here before we expected," he said. "We better be prepared for that. They have Indians with them so they may have picked up our trail when we left the desert. Probably not, but we have a lot riding on this."

Silvestra said, "The chief has set lookouts, but I'll watch too."

Sundance and Jorge were bunked in one of the empty stone houses. It was very cold even with a fire going. A thin night wind keened through the passageways between the abandoned buildings. The two men sat with blankets over their shoulders, working on their guns.

"It's funny how it comes back to you," Jorge said, jacking shells out of his Winchester .66. "This could be the same rifle I carried in the last year of the revolution. I remember the first small shipment of these rifles we got from the United States. Remember how we went to Vera Cruz and rowed out to the American ship lying off Punte del Norte. The French nearly got us on the way back to Juarez. Ah, a fine repeating rifle."

"I remember," Sundance said. "A hundred Winchesters, all brand new. That captain from New Orleans was well paid for them."

"But not more than they were worth," Jorge said. "Worth to the revolution. You picked the men to use those rifles and you taught them how to shoot to the best effect. The day they were sent out against the French at Las Animas. The French and their Mexican puppets came on in fine battle order, flags flying, drums rolling, confident that they were going to walk over the dirty Juaristas. On they came and then the charge was sounded. That was when those hundred Winchesters cut loose. It was a beautiful slaughter. I hope tomorrow's slaughter will be equally beautiful."

Sundance finished with his own rifle and slid it into its beaded and fringed scabbard. He prodded the loads out of his Colt .44. "For a so-called man of peace,

Jorge, you have the damnedest way of expressing yourself."

"Why not speak the truth? It was good to kill the French. It will be even better to ambush the slavers. My only regret is that Bannerman won't be with them. My hope would be to take him alive and throw him from the top of the mesa."

"I'd just settle for him dead," Sundance said. "Bannerman won't be along, but most of his little army will. We may not get another chance to get them all bunched together. That's why we have to make a good job of it—wipe them out to the last man."

"You think we can do it?"

"We'd better do it, or we're finished. If Bannerman gets most of his army back intact, we can forget about ever going back to Las Piedras. If we do kill all of them here, we can go back. For how long I don't know. Like I said, it will take Bannerman a while to recruit some new guns. Maybe we'll break him by then."

Jorge said quietly, "I would like to see that before I die."

Sympathy would have been out of place, so Sundance didn't offer any. They both knew that nothing could be done. It was only a matter of time before Jorge died. "We'll try to see that you get your wish," Sundance said quietly.

They stretched out on the packed dirt floor and slept for a few hours. Just before dawn Sundance heard someone coming. He cocked his gun. It was Silvestra. "They're coming," the big Indian said. "Many men."

Red light came through the doorway and streaked the dirt floor with vivid color. Sundance stood up.

"How long, Silvestra?"

"Thirty minutes, maybe less," Silvestra answered.

The big Indian was impassive as ever, but Sundance could feel the killing urge behind his eyes. There would be no mercy for any Bannerman rider who got in front of his gun.

They went outside and the chief was

there with the women and children. The children shivered in the cold wind blowing across the top of the mesa, and Sundance felt something of Silvestra's hatred for the slavers. The Pimas lived in peace with themselves and with nature, working hard for their meager prosperity —and now a bunch of men without souls were riding hell bent to destroy them. Yes, Sundance thought, it will be a pleasure to kill them.

"I know the women and children are frightened," Sundance told Silvestra, "but they will be all right. Tell the chief that. But tell the chief they must not run until the slavers can see them. They are to run into the abandoned houses, then out the other side. The slavers will run in after them and that's the last running they'll ever do."

The women had already started fires in the abandoned buildings, and now the smoke spiraled up from the chimneys— the beginning of another day in an Indian village. After the chief had been sent to join the men, Sundance, Jorge and

Silvestra took up their positions. Each of them had two sticks of dynamite, left over from setting charges in the houses. There was no need to tell Silvestra the length of fuse he should use.

Sundance took the two sticks from Jorge and fitted them with short fuses. "If I cut it much shorter it'll blow up in your hand," he said. "That means once it's lit, get rid of it fast. Don't decide where to throw it after you light it. Know where it's going to go before you light it. Get a cigar going when they start up the cliff, but keep another one handy in case they take too long to reach the top. Don't show yourself when the time comes—just throw it."

The three men took up their positions, Sundance flat on his belly in a clump of brush, Silvestra behind a jumble of rocks, Jorge in a narrow fissure that ran across the top of the mesa. While they waited the sun climbed up in the sky, flooding the mesa with light. At first it was red, then it turned blazing white.

Time passed and the air grew hot.

Waiting, the women were too silent, but the children made up for it. The younger ones were completely unaware that the destruction or survival of their small peaceful world depended on three strangers, men they had never seen before and would never see again after today.

The Indian lookout at the rim of the mesa turned suddenly and raised his fist in the air. Silvestra had told him to raise his hand once for every man in the raiding party. By the time he had finished he had raised and lowered his hand nineteen times. Silvestra waved him away from the rim and he ran silently to join the men.

Now everything was quiet except for the careless laughter of the children. The Pima village had stood atop this mesa for hundreds of years, protected by the desert from even the relentless Spaniards. Countless generations had lived and died here—always in peace. It was a strangely peaceful place for a massacre, Sundance thought.

Bannerman's men were coming up the face of the mesa. Sundance could hear them calling back and forth. He waited with his finger resting outside the trigger guard. A round was already in the chamber; all he had to do was line up the Winchester and fire. In the past he had killed many men who badly needed killing, but never had he felt such deadly intent as now.

The first man to reach the top of the mesa was an Indian, a short squat Apache with a red headband, carrying a brass-framed Winchester. Brass nails had been driven into the stock to make a decoration. The whole rifle seemed to glitter in the sun. The Pima children stopped laughing when they saw him, riveted in silence by his sinister presence. Sundance held his breath, hoping the women wouldn't panic and run too soon. They might have if the Apache hadn't turned away from them. He waved the other slavers to keep on coming.

One by one they appeared at the rim of the mesa. There were two other Apaches; the rest of the slavers were Americans and Mexicans. Sundance kept looking for the gunman called Cajun, but he wasn't among them. Now they were all on the mesa. They started forward in a bunch, cruel arrogant men already counting their profits.

The Apache spoke for the first time—and the Pimas ran toward the abandoned dwellings. They poured into the narrow passageways between the houses. They were already out of sight when the Apache fired a shot in the air, and the slavers followed at a dead run. Sundance blew the ash from the tip of his cigar and watched them run. They ran into the maze of passageways and doors. They were all inside except for three or four men when Sundance leveled the rifle and exploded the first charge. The women and children were running fast to safety when the first charge shook the top of the mesa. They all had their targets and the other charges went off as Jorge and Silvestra opened fire. The explosions flashed bright orange in the sunlight. Countless tons of stone and baked mud caved in on the trapped slavers. Sundance touched the tip of his cigar to a charge and threw it. The first stick of dynamite was still bouncing when he threw the second. Smoke and flame boiled up, and men screamed as they were shredded or crushed by falling debris. Through the man-made hell Sundance heard Jorge screaming out his rage. A man trying to hold in his guts came staggering from the ruins of one of the houses. Sundance shot him in the chest. Then he killed a man with most of his face blown away. This man had no eyes and he ran clawing the air, begging for mercy. A few slavers had broken through at the other end. Jorge and Silvestra cut them down in a hail of bullets. Inside the ruined dwellings men were still screaming, but there was no answering fire. Sundance jumped to his feet and saw Jorge and Silvestra coming from the other direction.

Jorge's normally sad eyes were wild with excitement. The killing mood was on him—the killing rage that comes only to quiet men who have been driven too far and for too long. He stopped and shot a

114

man who had managed to crawl out of the ruins with his shirt on fire. He shot the man again, though he was already dead.

"God forgive me, I am so happy!" he yelled.

Sundance took no notice of him. "I'll go after the others down below," he told Silvestra. "You stay here and kill the wounded, if there are any wounded. I have to catch up with the men down below before they get too much of a start."

Silvestra nodded. "Where will we find you, Sundance?"

"I'll wait for you," Sundance said.

"All right," Silvestra said and turned away.

Sundance's horse was saddled and ready to travel, with four full canteens of water slung from the pommel. Leading the great stallion to the edge of the mesa, he saw two men riding down the slope into the canyon, pushing their horses as fast as they could travel. They had a start on him, but there was no way to hurry. Going down was a lot more dangerous than coming up, and so he went carefully. He talked quietly to his mount, easing him over the worst places where the wall of the mesa fell straight down in an almost unbroken line. Up on the mesa an occasional shot rang out, but all firing had stopped before he was halfway to the bottom.

It took him twenty minutes to reach the floor of the canyon, and by then the two fleeing slavers had disappeared. They had about half an hour's start on him, but he felt no sense of impatience. He would follow them for as long as it took, and then he would kill them.

Going out through the draw to where the country ran down into the desert he watched for an ambush. When nobody shot at him he touched the big stallion's flanks with his moccasined feet and rode down the slope at a gallop. Panic had caused the two slavers to pass up the only good chance they had of taking him by surprise. He would see that they didn't get another.

Whoever the two men were, they were

moving fast, maybe too fast for the country that lay ahead. He eased the stallion to a walk when he reached broken country covered with rocks and sliding shale. Chipped rocks told him that the two slavers were going at a dangerous pace. He topped the last ridge before the desert flats began. Then he saw them far off in the distance, raising dust, moving fast. He knew with grim satisfaction that there was only one direction they could go and hope to stay alive—and that was back the way they had come. The journey east was a terrible one; north and south was worse.

A few miles into the desert he saw an empty canteen. Now that he was down on the flats he could no longer see their dust. He rode easily with his hat brim pulled low over his eyes to guard against the glare of the sun on the gypsum sand. Five miles out into the desert he spilled water into his hat and let the stallion drink. Then he swallowed a mouthful of water and mounted up again.

Now it was two hours later and the

stallion sensed death before he did. Sundance raised himself in the stirrups and shaded his eyes with his hand. Far off in the distance something big and black made a sharp contrast with the stark whiteness of a sand dune. He rode until he was about five hundred yards away, then dismounted and walked ahead with the rifle in his hands. The stallion followed, whinnying now and then.

A horse with a broken leg lay dying halfway up the dune, and Sundance didn't see the dead man until he got closer. The body was already partly covered with drifting sand. The dead man had been shot in the face; sand already caked the shredded cheekbone. Sundance went to the top of the dune and saw a dust cloud in the distance. No need to hurry now. He went back down then shot the dying horse. The animal kicked once and died. It was all written out as clear as day. One of the horses had broken a leg and there had been a short dispute about the other animal. The buzzards were already circling in, lighting down and flapping into the air again, getting closer all the time.

Sundance led the stallion over the crest of the dune and mounted up when he got to the other side. By now he had come more than twenty miles from the mesa, and the sun was well past the noon mark. In the distance, the dry lake stretched out like eternity.

He was less than a mile from it when he saw a riderless horse coming toward him. At first it was just a vague shape with a trail of dust behind it. It got closer. He pulled the Winchester from its scabbard and waited. Now he was close enough to see the dust-darkened froth dripping from the crazed animal's mouth. The animal's eyes bulged in terror and sweat glistened on its flanks. It galloped straight at him, and his own horse whinnied with fright. Sundance raised the Winchester, took careful aim and fired. The heavy bullet struck the maddened horse between the eyes, but the force of its gallop took the animal another ten or fifteen feet before its forelegs buckled abruptly and it fell in a heap.

No hurry now, Sundance thought. No hurry at all.

Out on the dry lake the last of the slavers was running and falling and getting up again. He got up after falling again and looked back at Sundance. The slaver fell again and got up again. He raised a rifle to his shoulder. The barrel of the rifle wavered this way and that. The first shot echoed out across the lake, but the bullet didn't even come close. Then with a wild, despairing scream the hunted man emptied the rifle as fast as he could work the lever. Bullets whined like hornets, but Sundance kept coming. Then it was time to get it over with. The slaver had dropped the rifle and was grabbing at his belt gun when Sundance shouldered the Winchester and shot him through the heart. The man fell without a sound. Sundance rode in close and shot him in the head. He knew it was a wasted bullet, but it was something he felt like doing.

After thumbing a fresh cartridge into the rifle, he rode back to the edge of the lake. Now there was nothing to do but wait.

7

"**T**HEY'LL eat the horses," Silvestra said on the way back across the desert. "The Pimas have never kept horses, not having any use for them, so they will eat those of the slavers. First, there will be a big feast, then the rest of the horse meat will be salted and stored away in a deep cave. Some of the meat will be dried in the sun, cut in strips and dried just like any other meat."

It all sounded good to Sundance. "And you left no doubt about the bodies?" he asked the big Indian.

"None at all. They were already stripping the bodies when we left. The clothes were to be burned and the bodies left out for the buzzards. Nineteen bodies at one time—the buzzards will think it is Christmas."

"And the guns?"

"Thrown down a crack in the rocks. It goes down hundreds of feet. No one will ever find them. The saddles were burned along with the clothes."

Jorge said, "And the whips, I burned the whips myself. Some of the whips still had dried blood on them. What I don't understand, Sundance, is why you're taking all this trouble to hide the fact that nineteen slavers were killed while trying to enslave a whole Pima village. I myself think it is news that should be spread far and wide. My message would be—if nineteen men are killed at a peaceful Pima village . . ."

"It wouldn't work the way you want it to," Sundance said. "Don't forget most of the slavers were whites and Mexicans. That makes a difference. It's all right for the whites and Mexicans to kill Indians, but an Indian isn't supposed to fight back, even in defense of his life or his home. If the story got out the state would be up in arms. They would call it a Pima uprising because few people know who the Pimas are, or where they have their villages. They would send soldiers in from the coast and destroy them even more completely than the slavers."

"It's hard to believe," Jorge said.

"It's true," Silvestra said. "Sundance speaks the truth. In time the story will get out somehow, and that will be good for the Pimas. By then the bones of the slavers will be bone dry, pounded to dust between stones, scattered to the wind. Nothing will remain except the rumor. It will make the Pimas stronger than if they had gone to war."

After days of traveling they were over the worst part of the journey back to Las Piedras. With no one pressing them from behind, they were able to travel at a better pace. This time they had taken along extra canteens and dried fruit given to them by the Pimas. In three days, if nothing happened, they would be in Las Piedras.

It was night and they were camped in a hollow that protected them from the wind blown dust. There was no longer any reason to go without a fire. On the fire a coffee pot, taken from one of the slavers, steamed in the cold night air. Silvestra crushed his hat and used it to take the coffee pot off its bed of coals. The coffee was Mexican—black and scalding hot.

Jorge chuckled over the rim of his tin cup. "Bannerman is going to be surprised when he hears I'm back. He'll be even more surprised when those twenty-one men of his don't show up with a load of Pima slaves. I've just had a thought that worries me. Suppose he sends out another large party to look for the missing men. If he does that the Pimas will be as badly off as they were."

Sundance was waiting for the coffee to cool. He set down the cup and put more dead wood on the fire. "That was a big expedition even for Bannerman," he said. "Now he doesn't have many men left, but even if he did have the men he wouldn't send them out into the desert. Bannerman is too smart for that. Besides, don't forget he used to be a brigadier and a pretty good one, I'm told. When those men fail to turn up, say in a week from now, he'll know something is wrong. Being a killer and a thief he'll probably figure that he's been double-crossed by his own men. He'll figure they have decided to go into business for themselves. Fifty or sixty Pima captives at four or five hundred a head, more if they take them south. Silvestra says in the haciendas north of Mexico City a healthy captive, fetches as much as a thousand dollars."

"Especially if the captive is a young girl, and pretty," Silvestra said. "In the fancy *burdels* of Mexico City a pretty Indian girl—and the women of the Pimas are comely girls—would easily fetch, as you say, the sum of one thousand dollars. I am speaking now of the *burdels* for rich men who fancy very young girls, even children. The keeper of such a *burdel* would get his investment back in less than a month. And I have heard stories of very young girls sold to women of a certain kind. There is a name for them, but I do not know what it is. Naturally, they too are rich. They will pay an even higher price if the girl is to their liking."

Sundance said, "All that will work in our favor, at least for a while. Bannerman will think his slavers have gone south with the Pima captives. He'll be too busy trying to track them down to bother with us. A man like Bannerman never learns to take a loss. He's vicious but above all he's greedy. No matter how much money or power he gets, it will never be enough."

Jorge said, "You sound as if you think he will be around for a long time."

"No, it was just a way of speaking. Bannerman will never give up so the only way is to kill him. I don't know yet how that can be done, but it is the only way. He is well guarded. Colonel Almirante is on his payroll and, through the colonel, he has the protection of the Mexican Army. If we don't kill Bannerman, we can expect to die at some point. Not now because he'll be too busy trying to track down his lost expedition. It will take time to do that, but Colonel Almirante will be of much service. Army posts to the south will be instructed to watch for a large party of heavily armed men with Indian captives. Then day by day word will come back to Bannerman—no slavers, no Indians. When enough reports like that get back to him he will know what really happened to his men. That's why we have to use what time we have, and use it well."

"Do you have a plan?" Jorge asked. He finished the last of the coffee in the pot.

"No, not yet," Sundance answered. "But we better come up with something before Bannerman gets to the truth."

Jorge asked, "How do you think it'll be when we get back to town? I'm supposed to be halfway to Morelos."

"We better stick together," Sundance said. "I figure Bannerman will be too busy to bother with you for a while. Unless I'm wrong you'll be unfinished business, something that has to be taken care of but not right away. Anyway, he doesn't have the men to spread around."

Jorge lay down and rolled himself in his blanket. His face was turned away from the others. "Do you think we're going to win, Sundance?" he asked. "Late at night I sometimes think of what's waiting for me, what I have to face before too long. I don't want to go but I can face it if I know we're going to win."

Sundance never lied and he refused to lie now even if it meant comfort to a dying friend. "We have a good chance," he said. "All we can give this fight is our best."

Two weeks after leaving Las Piedras they were back there. At a waterhole five miles from town they washed off the dust of travel. They sluiced water over the horses and let them rest for half a day. Fingering his stubbly face, Jorge said, "I think I'll grow a beard. I don't know if I'll be able to hack off this growth of barbed wire."

Jorge had washed his face and slicked back his long black hair. He used a wet bandanna to wipe the dust from his hat and boots. "How do I look?" he asked Sundance.

Sundance smiled. "Like you've been for a ride in the country."

"That's it," Jorge said. "I've been on a picnic."

Jorge turned his horse over to Silvestra when they came to the place, a small canyon, where the wagon and wagon horse were hidden. The wagon horse had been left to graze on a long rope, cared for by one of Silvestra's friends while they'd been away.

After they hitched up the wagon, Jorge climbed up on the seat. "Here's where I go back to being a lawyer," he said, and picked up the reins.

"I'll ride in ahead of you," Sundance said. "If there is going to be trouble for you, I'd like to know about it. Come on in if I don't ride out to stop you. Silvestra, you ride along with Jorge."

The big Indian nodded. "You watch yourself too."

It was about noon when Sundance rode into Las Piedras. It was hot and quiet except for the cries of the street vendors. It was close to siesta time and the town was drowsy. A hot wind blew dust against the walls of the houses. A troop of cavalry trotted through town, heading north.

Sundance crossed the plaza, then rode the stallion down the narrow street to where Jorge had his quarters. Loungers in doorways gave him curious looks though some of them had seen him before. There was no sign of any of Bannerman's men. Sundance hitched his horse to an iron ring in the wall and went up to Jorge's rooms. The door was open and he went in. The neighbors had been there. The furniture, such as it was, had been taken away, and so had the cook-stove and all the pots and pans.

It would be about an hour before Jorge got to town, so Sundance used the time to ask at the hotel if there had been any more telegraph messages from General Crook. "No, nothing," the proprietor said uneasily. "You have not been in your room, Señor Sundance. You have paid for your fine room, but you have not been in it. If a message had come from your friend, the general, I would not have

131

known where to find you. And if one should come now?"

Sundance told the hotel keeper where he could be found, then went to the store kept by the German on the plaza. "You are my best customer," the German said.

Jorge and Silvestra came riding in at fifteen minutes after one. News that the trouble-making lawyer was back ran through the town; siesta was forgotten. Men from the cantinas pushed out onto the sidewalk to gape at the sickly, mescal-soaked attorney who had dared to stand up to Lucas Bannerman. Sundance had stabled his horse and was standing in the plaza when Jorge's wagon came into sight. Silvestra rode beside the wagon, a few feet behind Jorge. Jorge was enjoying himself a little too well, Sundance thought, but maybe he had earned it.

There was more than a little of the actor in Jorge, for as he passed Sundance he doffed his hat and said in a loud voice, "How are you, Señor Sundance, and how has this fair city been during my absence?"

Sundance couldn't help smiling. "Everybody missed you," he said.

A little later Jorge was not so cheerful; in fact, he was in a murderous rage. He paced the room kicking empty bean cans out of his way. Sundance and Silvestra waited for him to finish his tirade. That took a while.

"Those dogs!" he raged. "To steal a man's cookstove!"

Sundance smiled at Silvestra. "What's the difference, Jorge? You never cooked anything anyway. All right, you made coffee, if you want to call it that."

But his smile faded when he saw the sweat beading on Jorge's face. A few hours earlier he had looked all right—almost healthy—but now his face was drained of color. His skin looked dead and his hands shook. The wild rage over the stolen stove was just part of it.

Sundance unrolled blankets and spread them on the floor. "You have to lie down," he said. "You have to rest. Silvestra will stay and I will get you a drink."

Jorge wiped his face with his sleeve. "I don't want a drink and I'll soon get all the rest I need. The sickness attacks me and I go a little crazy. It doesn't last. It never lasts."

"Don't be a fool," Sundance said. "Lie down and rest. I'll get a bed in here and you can sleep."

Jorge refused to listen. "I am not a woman to be pampered," he said. "I didn't fail you out there in the desert, did I? You thought—you too, Silvestra—you thought you would have to carry me on your back. But you were wrong. Admit you were wrong."

Sundance said he was glad to be wrong. "Jorge, if you need a drink I will go for a bottle. If a drink will help I'll get it for you."

Jorge shook his head wearily. His eyes were still bright with the sickness and would finally kill him, but now he was calmer. "No drink," he said. "I worked too hard on that cure to start drinking again. I'm all right, I can get along without the mescal. Bannerman said my brain was rotted by mescal, but I will show him how wrong he was."

"You're right," Sundance said. "You feel well enough to talk about Bannerman? What we should do next?"

"You mean, have I stopped acting like a crazy man?"

"Something like that. We bought some time out there on that mesa. How much is anybody's guess. You still haven't given up the idea of using the law to beat him, have you?"

"How did you know?"

"That last day coming back you didn't talk at all. You mind telling me what you have in mind?"

Jorge smiled and began to unpack the law books they had brought up from the wagon. "Not tonight. In the morning I'll be ready to talk about it. Tonight I have much reading to do."

"All right," Sundance said, "but we better keep a watch on Bannerman's *rancheria*. Could be he'll move against us sooner than we think. We have to be ready for anything he can throw at us.

Silvestra can stay here with you while I scout the country."

The big Indian picked up his rifle. "No," he said in his formal way, "you stay here and I will scout the *rancheria*. I have done it many times and know all the ways to get in and out without being seen. I will keep watch and report back what I have seen. With your permission, Sundance, that is the best way to do it."

"He's right," Jorge said, taking one of the law books from the stack on the floor.

Silvestra was at the door.

"How long will you be gone?" Sundance asked him.

"Maybe a few days."

Sundance said, "Watch yourself all the time you're out there. Bannerman will be in a killing mood when he figures out what happened to his men."

After Silvestra left Sundance bolted the door and checked the twin loads in the Greener shotgun. "Wake me if you hear anything—anything at all," he told Jorge. "I'm going to sleep for a while."

The tall halfbreed stretched out on the

floor and was instantly asleep. During the night we woke up several times, but it was nothing more than Jorge getting up to stretch his legs. By the time the first light slanted through the windows, the lawyer was still writing rapidly on long yellow sheets of legal paper. Sundance looked out at the street, but it was silent and empty except for a starved mongrel pawing at something in the gutter.

Jorge continued to write furiously while Sundance opened a can of peaches and drank some of the juice. "I think it will work," he said, throwing down his pen. His pants were spattered with ink. "It has to work."

"What?" Sundance speared a peach slice with the point of his knife.

Jorge's dark eyes were excited but no longer feverish. "I think I've found a way to put Bannerman out of the slaving business. When I was out there in the desert I remembered an old law that nobody remembers any more. I wasn't sure I was right, so I didn't say anything.

Now I'm sure. Some of the south-western tribes were Mexican nationals before the Mexican War. After the war all Mexican citizens who remained in the territory taken by the United States automatically became American citizens. That means many of the captives Bannerman has been taking are United States citizens. Don't you understand?"

"I know what you're telling me," Sundance said.

"No! No! Listen to me," Jorge said impatiently, pounding his fist on one of the law books. "If some of the Indian captives are American citizens, they are entitled to the same protection as any other American citizen. Maybe the Indians don't know about this old law, or have forgotten it, but I will prove it to be a fact of law. I will go into the courts, I will go to the Governor of Sonora, to President Diaz if I have to."

Sundance said, "I thought you tried all that?"

"Ah, but now it's different. This time the American government is involved. I will go to Washington if I have to. How can they ignore it?"

"It wouldn't be easy," Sundance agreed. "Even if Bannerman is tied in with the Indian Ring, he'd find it hard to get away with kidnaping American citizens. Where will you start first?"

Sundance was heartened by the look in his old friend's eyes. It would be good if Jorge could die knowing that his life had been worth something. Other dying men might have found that small comfort, but Sundance knew how Jorge felt about it.

"Yes, the courts," Jorge answered, "and I will write a strongly-worded letter to the governor at the same time."

Sundance asked what the provincial judge was like. "If Bannerman has him on his payroll, your legal arguments will run into a stone wall."

Jorge didn't think so and explained why. "Judge Mendoza is a mean and miserable old man. But that doesn't say that he isn't honest. The biggest drawback is he's so old. I don't know how old, maybe eighty-five. He's almost deaf so everything has to be presented in writing because he can't hear. But, in the end, I think he is a good and fair judge. I never heard otherwise. Oratory means nothing to him—you have to write it out and it has to be as clear and simple as you can make it."

Jorge gathered up the sheaf of ink-spattered legal sheets from the floor. "What I have written here is just the beginning. I will have to write it again and again until it is right. Judge Mendoza can be very impatient."

"How long will it take to finish?"

"Days, two or three days, maybe as long as a week. I know you are thinking about Bannerman, so I will say four days. I'm going to need a table to work on."

Sundance said, "The German on the plaza sells everything. I guess he carries tables too. I'm going to get some charcoal so we can make coffee in the fireplace and fry some meat. Anything else you want?"

"A bottle of benzene," Jorge said, "to clean my clothes and my hat before I go into Judge Mendoza's court. A lawyer with a dirty suit wouldn't last long with the old man. And some yellow soap to wash my shirt."

Sundance was unbolting the door. "That shirt is past washing—I'll get you a new one. Keep the door bolted while I'm gone."

"I feel so good about all this," Jorge said before Sundance went down to the street.

"Sure," Sundance said. He had been around too long to put much faith in anything but his weapons. They never failed you if you knew how to use them right.

8

JORGE worked furiously for the next three days, mumbling to himself as the steel-nibbed pen raced across page after page of legal paper. The small cheap pine table Sundance had bought from the German storekeeper was already stained with ink and ringed with drippings from coffee cups. The floor was littered with crumpled sheets of paper and there was always the smell of coffee in the two small rooms. Jorge hardly slept at all and Sundance gave up telling him he ought to. They ate bacon and eggs and steak and beans—all cooked over charcoal in the stone fireplace. Silvestra hadn't come back from scouting Bannerman's ranch.

Sundance whiled away the time by working on his weapons. Northern Mexico was a waterless country with dust always in the wind. The fine, gritty dust seeped through everything, even the best gun cover. General Crook hadn't sent any more telegrams. Sundance, hunkered down on the floor, wiped gun oil from the muzzle of the 44–40 Winchester. Any gun had a tendency to throw wild if you didn't wipe oil from the muzzle. After he finished with the Winchester he got a small slab of soapstone from his warbag and put an even finer edge on the Bowie knife. He moistened the stone and stroked the knife blade across it, shifting the angle of the blade as the edge grew keener. When he was satisfied that the great fighting knife was in perfect condition, he took the rag soaked in gun oil and wiped the blade clean and replaced it in its sheath. Working on his weapons, the tools of his trade, relaxed him, but there was more to it than making work to pass the time. A man was only as good as his weapons and not a week went by that he didn't practice with all of his weapons, especially the great ash bow that could kill an enemy in almost total darkness without making a sound. With a quiver of arrows slung over his back, he could kill men running toward him almost as quickly as he could knock them down with a repeating rifle. It was the weapon of his boyhood, the first one he had learned to use—it always felt natural and easy in his hands. The bow was an even more sensitive weapon than a gun because the bowstring had to be adjusted if the bow hadn't been used for some time. The temperature of the place he was in had to be considered, too.

Jorge, pen in one hand, a cup of cold coffee in the other, paused to look over at him. "If I win this case, and I will, you won't have to use those weapons. Not in Las Piedras."

Sundance had saved the big Remington for last. Every time he looked at the big-bore hunting rifle he thought of Lucas Bannerman. The thought refused to leave his head, but he hadn't said anything to Jorge.

"That's good," he told Jorge. "I'm all for law and order when I run into it. I'd be glad to save my bullets for the *tigres* in the Sierra."

Jorge didn't say anything for a few minutes. Then he said quietly, "I have never thanked you for helping me in this fight. This isn't even your country. But I thank you."

"No need for thanks," Sundance said. "I am half Cheyenne and I help the Indians any way I can. An Indian has no country except his family, his tribe, his own nation. Nothing is written down. A man has honor or he has not. So I help my mother's people wherever I can. It is the Indians who should thank you."

"I don't need thanks either. I am doing this thing, fighting this fight for myself. I just hope I can last long enough to get it done. I don't want to die but that would make the dying easier."

"You can't do everything, Jorge. No man can."

"I know that now."

"I was like you were when I began my fight against the Indian Ring," Sundance said. "Later I knew I was trying to do too much. I know now that the fight won't be won in my lifetime. Far from it but no matter. Other good men will go on fighting. General Crook is like that. He's a better man than I will ever be."

"Never," Jorge protested. "You are what we Mexicans call *raro*, a very rare man. No one is better than you are."

"Crook is. Better than me, better than you, better than most men."

Jorge smiled. "I don't mind not being so great as your general. You think he will come to Las Piedras, and will he help us when he comes?"

"He can't help officially, but the general has a way of cutting through red tape. The Indians respect him because he fights them hard when he has to but treats them fairly when he has won. A lot of politicians in Washington hate him and would like to destroy him because he sees them as the scum they are. He pulls a lot of weight because he never breaks his word once he gives it."

"I hope he comes soon," Jorge said, dipping his pen in the inkwell.

Sundance nodded agreement. "So do I."

On the evening of the fourth day Jorge threw down his pen and shuffled his papers into an orderly pile. His eyes were red-rimmed and his hollow cheeks were grown over with stubble. When he moved his head, he grimaced with pain. A skillet with a steak in it was sizzling on a bed of charcoal and beside it a pot of coffee steamed. Sundance opened a can of tomatoes, not saying anything because Jorge was reading over the final draft of what he had taken four days to write.

Sundance took the skillet off the fire and put the tomatoes on to heat. Silvestra hadn't come back. Now this was the fourth day he had been gone and it was beginning to look bad. Sundance hadn't mentioned his concern to Jorge, who had been buried in his law books and papers for the best part of a week. Silvestra, always a reliable man, was taking too long and for Sundance the bad feeling grew stronger with every minute that passed.

He knew there was nothing he could do but wait. Sundance dished up his half of the steak and started on it without waiting for Jorge who muttered as he read and scratched his head with the end of the pen at the same time. When he had finished, he folded the papers. He put them in a long brown envelope and wrote on the outside of it. Only then did he seem to see Sundance, the cooling steak and the pot of steaming coffee.

"It's finished," he said. "I don't know if there's anything I can add to it." Jorge had lost track of time. "What day is it?"

"The evening of the fourth day," Sundance answered.

Jorge looked surprised, then worried. "Why hasn't Silvestra returned? He said he'd be gone only a few days. Four days is too long."

Sundance poured coffee for Jorge who wasn't showing much interest in his steak. The coffee had cooked too long on the charcoal and it was ink black and bitter, the way Sundance liked it. He said, "If he isn't back by morning I'm going out to look for him."

Jorge's voice tried to sound confident. "Silvestra is a good man and can take care of himself. He'll be all right."

Thinking of all the good men he had known who were dead, Sundance said, "We'll wait till morning. Some of Bannerman's Apaches may have spotted him."

"Not Silvestra."

"It's possible. Anything is possible."

Jorge's hands trembled as he pushed the plate away from him. Grease was congealing on the plate and his coffee was getting cold. "If Bannerman's Apaches got him—it makes me sick to think about it."

"Wait until morning—don't think about it. No matter what happens to Silvestra you have to go ahead with your case. It's all that matters."

"To hell with my case. I don't give a damn about the case—I'm thinking about Silvestra."

"So am I, but there's nothing to be

done this time of night. Now get some sleep before I rap you over the head and lay you out. If you don't sleep soon, you won't be worth a damn to anybody. You hear what I'm telling you?"

But Jorge was already nodding in his chair and close to falling off it. Sundance got up quickly and helped him to the cot he had bought from the German. Then he pulled off Jorge's boots and, after the lawyer muttered something, he fell asleep again.

Sundance drank what was left of the coffee and sat down to wait for Silvestra to come back—if he ever came back. While the white half of him hoped that Silvestra would get back safely, the Indian half knew instinctively that the big Indian was dead. There was no way to explain it, but the knowledge was there, defying him to ignore it. In the past he had been wrong or mistaken—never about death—and when he picked up the heavy Remington rifle he thought about Bannerman again. It was hot in the little room and the town was quiet except for an occasional drunkard staggering home from the cantinas. While he sat and waited in silence, Jorge slept the half-dead sleep of a man who had come close to total exhaustion. It was a long night and the hours passed slowly, but he waited without impatience, listening for sounds.

He felt bad about Silvestra, but there was nothing that could be done about his death. In the end, this was Jorge's fight and he had to be given his chance to win it in his own way. Despite all the men he had killed in his time, Sundance did not consider himself a lawless man but simply a man who killed when the law was weak or corrupt and killing was the only way to right a wrong that would otherwise go unpunished. If the law failed again—that is, failed Jorge—he would take the big Remington and, in spite of all the odds against doing it, he would find a way to kill Lucas Bannerman. No man living could keep from being killed if the man who wanted to kill him had enough determination and was willing to die himself in the attempt.

Dawn was about three hours away when he heard footsteps coming up the stone stairs from the street. Sundance turned down the light, picked up the scattergun and thumbed back the twin hammers. Then he moved to one side of the door and waited for the footsteps to get to the top of the stairs.

There was no mistaking the voice outside when he heard it. It was a distinctive voice: Chief Police Luis Montoya had a sort of rattle in his throat when he talked, and the sound would have been hard to imitate.

"What do you want?" Sundance said without opening the door.

"Open the door," Montoya ordered. "I have something to tell you."

Sundance had his hand on the bolt. "You'd better be Luis Montoya and you better not have any of Bannerman's men with you."

Montoya said, "I am alone. Now open the door."

When the door was open and Montoya saw the shotgun he said angrily, "There is no need for that. I am Chief of Police of this town and you will not threaten me with guns of any kind."

"Nobody's threatening you," Sundance said, holding the shotgun steady as Montoya came in and looked around. "What do you want?"

Montoya took a deep breath. "The Indian is dead. The one called Silvestra is dead."

Jorge woke up when he heard Silvestra's name. He threw the blanket aside and got up with difficulty. His face was slick with sweat and his hair was matted and streaky. "What's this about Silvestra?" he said. "What were you saying about my friend?"

Jorge's eyes were so crazed that the police chief took a step backward before he remembered who he was. "He's dead," he said. "Your friend the Indian is dead. I came to tell you."

Jorge yelled, "You're a liar."

"Let him talk," Sundance said, pushing Jorge back with the flat of his hand. "Say the rest of it, Chief. If he's dead, where is he?"

He knew Montoya wasn't lying, wasn't part of a plan to lead them into a trap. The truth was in Montoya's voice and in his eyes.

"He's down in the street roped to his horse. I was at home sleeping when one of my men came banging on the door with news of a dead Indian tied to a horse in the plaza. When I got there I knew his face and his name, so I brought him here."

Jorge lunged at Montoya. Sundance pushed him away and kept him away while the police chief told what he knew. "All I know is that Indian is dead. I don't know who did it, or where it happened—what good would it do if I did? No court would hang the men who did it or even send them to prison. You blame me for not knowing what to do, but I will tell you what you should have done. You should have gone back to Morelos and stayed there. The Indian was here after you left and no one harmed him. No one harmed him because you were gone and it looked like the trouble was over. Then for your own crazy reasons you came back—and the Indian is dead. You spout from your damned law books—and it is the Indian who is dead."

Jorge looked at the floor in silence. Sundance said, "How did he die?"

"The worst way a man can die. In all my life—and I have been a soldier—I have seen nothing like it. *Madre de Dios,* such a way for a man to die. I ask you again: do you want to claim the body?"

The three men went down to the dark street to look at what had once been a man. The body lay across the saddle, wrists roped to ankles, covered with a blanket. Sundance guessed the blanket was Montoya's idea. The corpse smelled very bad.

The body began to slide when Sundance cut the ropes. He grabbed it before it hit the ground. When he took his hands away, they were slick with congealing blood. He wiped his hands on the blanket and knelt beside what was left of Silvestra. Jorge leaned against the wall of the building and vomited until nothing came up but air. Montoya didn't say anything until after he lit a cigar to kill some of the smell.

Then he said, "That's what they did to him. You are as much to blame as the lawyer, Señor Sundance."

Sundance didn't answer and Montoya didn't offer to help with the body. It was hard to know what to make of the Mexican policeman. Maybe he was an honest man after all. Time might tell what he was, but right then he was just an aging lawman blowing out clouds of cigar smoke to hide the stink.

In the dim light of the street, Sundance saw that Montoya was right about one thing—Silvestra had died in the worst possible way. The fingers and toes had been burned off and they hadn't stopped after they castrated him. Someone with a razor sharp knife had opened his belly from hip to hip. In his chest were many bullet holes, but Sundance decided the shooting had been done after he was dead.

They hadn't touched the face. There wasn't a mark on it, but even now it was contorted in agony, as if the corpse could still feel unbearable pain.

Sundance stood up and turned away from the body. It wasn't his place to say what should be done. Montoya was still puffing on the cigar, looking at nothing. Jorge was still close to the wall, pressing his forehead against the cool stone. A few Mexicans stood in the gloom of a doorway, watching silently. When a mongrel came sniffing its way to the body, Montoya kicked it savagely and it ran away howling. It was the police chief's only display of emotion.

Jorge's back was still turned. Sundance said, "What do you want to do? Bury him as he is? It doesn't make any difference."

"No, we will not bury him as he is!" Jorge's voice began loud and shrill. "We will bury him properly as a man should be buried." Jorge looked at Sundance and didn't seem to know him. "I will bury him myself if I have to."

Sundance nodded and Jorge threw a

silver dollar at one of the Mexicans in the doorway. "Here, you"—his voice was stronger now—"go and tell Camacho the undertaker to bring a coffin here." He came over and looked down at Silvestra's mutilated body. The smell didn't bother him.

"I knew that man, that damned Indian," he said to no one. "And now he's dead and I the one who should be dead am still alive." Jorge began to tremble again but now it was anger instead of sickness.

"You better go easy, Jorge," Sundance said, coming close.

Jorge shook off Sundance's arm and continued to stare at the body. "No, I won't go easy. The man who did this will pay for it. On my dead mother's grave, he will pay for this."

Montoya spoke quietly to Sundance. "Listen to how he talks. If you are his friend, why don't you take him away from this town? Make him see that what he's thinking won't do any good. It can only get him killed."

"Is that what you think, Montoya?"

"I'm saying it can only get him killed."

"You know Bannerman ordered this?"

The chief of police shrugged and threw his cigar away. Then he lit another. "What does it matter what I know? There is no way he can get close to Bannerman, and even if he did manage to kill him, he would hang for it."

"Maybe he thinks it's worth it."

"And what do you think?"

Sundance said, "I think it might be worth it."

"Worth it to you," Montoya said angrily.

"Worth it to Jorge. He has nothing to lose and at least Bannerman would be dead. The Indian was his closest friend, maybe his only real friend. I know how he feels."

"Then you won't make him leave Las Piedras?"

"I wouldn't make him even if I could."

Down the street an ancient hearse creaked out of a stable. The stableman, Camacho, made coffins and buried people when he wasn't tending to horses. The battered hearse was pulled by two mules and in the back of it was a cheap, brightly varnished coffin. As a stableman, Camacho wore a torn palm leaf hat; now he wore a rusty topper with crepe twisted around it. He was old and sleepy, with a soggy cigar in his mouth. He reined in the mules and climbed down from the driver's seat. The coffin was so cheap and light that he was able to lift it out of the hearse without any help. The mules stood patiently, their long ears twitching away flies.

"*Dios!*" he said when he saw what had been done to the body. "Who is *that?*"

The lid of the coffin had nails driven halfway in. The undertaker took the feet and Sundance the shoulders and they put Silvestra in the coffin. Then the undertaker got a hammer from the back of the hearse and nailed the lid down tight. The noise of the hammer on the lid sent echoes rolling through the town. Sundance and the undertaker slid the coffin into the hearse—the undertaker closed

160

the doors. By the time all this was done the night sky was streaked with red, but the town was still asleep as the hearse moved off toward the cemetery. The mules knew the way because it was a slow and familiar journey. They got to the plaza and crossed it in the shadow of the cathedral. Then the hearse turned into a long, narrow street lined with stores and cantinas on both sides. The dying moon shone on tin cans rusting in the gutter. The hearse went slowly and they walked silently behind it.

They went through the cemetery gates. Some of the graves had marble headstones and some homemade wooden crosses. Some of the marble memorials were decorated with carvings of angels and lambs. The hearse stopped and the undertaker got down with a shovel in his hand. He dug in the sandy soil until Sundance took the shovel away from him because he was taking too long. He stopped digging when he was down five feet; five feet was enough because the dogs wouldn't root down that far.

Sundance and the undertaker let the coffin down on ropes. Then the undertaker picked up the shovel and prepared to fill in the grave.

"Stand back. You're not burying a dog," Jorge said angrily.

Finally, it was over and they were leaving the cemetery. Jorge walked by himself. Montoya said to Sundance, "I urge you again, Señor Sundance. In the name of God, leave Las Piedras and take the lawyer with you. I don't want to have to bury both of you. You are up against men—a man—too powerful to stop. It can't be done. Don't you see that? There is nothing I can do. There is nothing anyone can do."

Sundance's voice was hard and cold. "Just don't take sides, Montoya. Stay neutral and you'll probably hang onto your job. You've been offering all kinds of good advice. Now I'll give you some—keep out of it."

"My advice is still good advice," the police chief said, not wanting to look at the hard lines of the other man's face.

"Sure," Sundance said. "You're full of good advice."

Then he quickened his pace to catch up with Jorge.

163

9

THEY walked in silence until they were halfway across the plaza. Then Jorge spoke and there was no feeling in his voice. "I am going to have a drink, a lot of drinks. Don't try to stop me, Sundance."

On the plaza stores and cantinas were opening for the business of the day. An old man leading a wagon loaded with chickens in crates cursed his mule for not going fast enough. Dwarfed by the great doors of the cathedral, an old priest with long white hair stood reading from a prayer book.

"What you do is your business," Sundance said. He waited outside a cantina while Jorge went in and came out with two bottles of mescal.

Jorge uncorked a bottle with his teeth and drank from it, shuddering as the raw spirit went down. "I have to think," he

164

said. "Silvestra's death has changed everything."

They walked on and Sundance let him talk. Jorge said, "I despise Montoya, but he's right. So I despise myself even more. What did Montoya say? I spout from my damned law books, but it is the Indian who is dead. Silvestra, the Indian, is dead —and what am I going to do about it?"

Now they were back in Jorge's quarters and a good part of the first bottle was gone. Jorge sat down heavily and swept the law books off the table with his arm. He set down the bottles and pointed to the long-barreled Colt holstered at Sundance's side. "You were right too," he said bitterly. "Right when you said only guns can settle this. Everybody is right but me. You, Montoya—everybody except Jorge Calderon, the great advocate and champion of the Indians."

Jorge spilled mescal on his shirt as he drank. When he saw what he had done, he laughed again. "My new shirt, my new clean shirt," he said, already half drunk. "What the hell does it matter? Won't be needing it. Don't need to wear a clean shirt to kill a man. All this time I've been blind or maybe I didn't have the nerve. I studied my law books and thought the answer was there. Then I wrote letters to the newspapers and got up petitions—and all the time the answer was right in front of my nose."

"You mean killing Lucas Bannerman."

"That's it—kill Bannerman."

Jorge took another swig of mescal, this time without shuddering. "I changed it back," he said. "What happened to Silvestra made me change it back."

"You think you're going to kill Bannerman. Tell me how."

"I won't talk. This time I won't talk—I'll do it. Bannerman is a man so he can be killed like any other man."

"No, not just like any other man. He's tough, smart and well guarded. You won't even get close to him. All you'll do is get killed. His pistoleros will gun you down before you get off a shot. Where will that leave your case?"

"Shit on the case!" Jorge drank again

and smashed the empty bottle against the wall. "I'll get to him and I'll kill him. I think I'll go and kill him now."

Sundance got between Jorge and the door. "Not a chance," he said. "Drink all you want, but you're not leaving. I'll rope you if I have to."

Suddenly Jorge's eyelids began to droop and his voice began a mumble. "All right! All right!" he said. Then before Sundance could close the distance between them Jorge grabbed up the scatter-gun. "Stay back"—he was swaying on his feet—"I'm warning you, stay back!"

Sundance crowded in on him. Jorge reversed the shotgun and tried to hit him with the stock. Sundance grabbed the shotgun and drew his belt gun at the same time. He hated to do it, but it was time for Jorge to sleep off this craziness, so as gently as he could he tapped him on the back of the neck with the barrel of the Colt. Jorge's eyes closed and he sagged forward. He would have fallen if Sundance hadn't caught him easily with one hand. Then he carried Jorge over to the cot and covered him with blankets after taking off his coat and boots. Before he had finished Jorge began to snore.

Late in the afternoon Jorge woke up with a headache and a stiff neck. He didn't remember and Sundance didn't explain. Sundance poured a half glass of mescal and held it while he drank. "Drink this and that's the end of the drinking," Sundance ordered.

"What happened last night?" Jorge asked, finishing the mescal in two convulsive swallows. "I remember starting on the first bottle. After that it's all confusion in my mind. Then I must have fallen asleep."

Sundance went to the window and poured out the rest of the mescal. "That's what happened," he said. "You fell asleep."

Jorge lay back on the cot and closed his eyes. When he spoke his eyes were still closed. It was coming back to him. "I wanted to kill Bannerman—to try to kill Bannerman—and you stopped me. I still hunger to kill him. It isn't right to let him get away with this."

"Sober up, clean yourself and get ready for Judge Mendoza. That's how you can get Bannerman. You can't get him for killing Silvestra, but maybe you can send him to jail. In the end you may have to settle for putting him out of business. Are you ready to settle for that?"

"Yes," Jorge said after thinking about it, "I would settle for that. And if I should fail . . ."

"If the law fails you, we'll find a way to kill Bannerman," Sundance said. "But you have to give the law a chance."

"One more chance," Jorge said. "Silvestra was a good and brave man."

"I know he was."

"He was gentle for a man of such great strength. A strange man in many ways."

"He had no family of any kind?"

Jorge said, "No one. All dead. The Franciscan monks found him after the Mexican cavalry swept through his village. All his life he was so proud he could read and write. It's terrible that he had to die like that."

There was nothing to say, so Sundance didn't say anything.

Judge Esteban Mendoza held court in Las Piedras on the first Monday of every month. To get there he had to be driven in a private coach from the provincial capital at Durango. It was a two-day journey with a stopover on the way, but in all the years he had been coming to Las Piedras, he had never missed a day in court. His day in court was a long one, from eight in the morning until far into the evening. The old man's decisions were swift and final.

"He's going to die in court or on the way to court," Jorge told Sundance. It was Sunday afternoon and he was sponging his black suit with benzene. The pungent smell of the benzene filled the small room, driving out the smells of cooking. Sundance smiled as Jorge, never a deft man with his hands, scrubbed away at the sweatstained collar of his coat.

170

Jorge had washed his mescal-soaked shirt and hung it over the back of a chair to dry. Monday was only hours away and Jorge wanted to look his best.

"Mendoza dismissed all my other cases," Jorge said, "and maybe he was right. 'Your arguments are unsound, Señor Calderon,' he said to me more than once. Well, we'll see what he has to say this time. What he decides should tell what he's really like. Throw my hat over here, will you. I'd buy a new one but the stores won't open on Sunday. *Dios!* That trip across the desert didn't do it any good."

Sundance reminded him that he wouldn't be wearing his hat in court. "Take it easy, Jorge. You'll be all right. A good night's sleep and you'll be fine."

"Where the hell is the boot blacking?"

"On the table right in front of you."

"You notice I'm saving the worst part for last," Jorge said, rubbing the quarter-inch stubble on his face.

Jorge soaked his face in a hot towel, then lathered it energetically. Sundance had sharpened his razor for him until it was sharp enough to slice through a hair, but even so it took fifteen minutes to get the whiskers off.

Later, Sundance cooked a steak and by then it was eight o'clock. Jorge looked at his watch after he wound it with a key. "Only twelve hours to go. *Dios!* I would like it to be Tuesday. It's been so quiet —no sign of any of Bannerman's riders."

"If they're out there, I didn't see them," Sundance said. "I think Bannerman is waiting to see what your next move will be. Now you better turn in and I'll do the same."

"Who the hell is able to sleep on a night like this?" Jorge said, but as it turned out he slept very well.

In the morning Jorge refused everything but coffee. It was seven o'clock. The walk to the courthouse took only five minutes, but Jorge wanted to get there early. "It will calm me just to be there," he said. "I can sit there and think of all the centuries of law and that calms me."

"Let's go then." Sundance smiled. "So you can be calm."

The courthouse was on the west side of the plaza, now crowded with vendors, beggars and farmers. The two men—the frail Mexican lawyer and the rangy half-breed fighting man—were conscious of the stares that followed them. The sun was already hot, straw and dust blew in the wind. To the east, jutting up into the clear blue sky, was the jagged outline of the Sierra Madre. Sundance looked at the great mountain range with a sudden longing to be there, high up in the cool mountain air and far away from towns, men and killing. Up on the highest peaks it was cold even in the hottest part of summer. There were clear, cold streams where the water was good to drink. It would be good when this was over, to go there with Crook, to sit by a campfire in the cool of the evening, waiting for fish to broil over an open fire.

"There it is," Jorge said, "the temple of law."

The courthouse was the grandest

building in Las Piedras after the cathedral. It was three stories and built of cut stone. Over it flew the flag of the Republic of Mexico and the state flag of Sonora. Stone steps led up to the massive doors, which were guarded by two soldiers with rifles and serious expressions on their brown Indian faces. Lawyers and their clerks and clients were gathered in knots in front of the building and on the steps leading up to it. Sundance saw Chief of Police Montoya talking to two of his blue-uniformed constables.

Before they reached the courthouse Bannerman, the gunman called Cajun and two Mexican pistoleros rode up and hitched their horses. They went inside. "It's all right," Jorge said. "I'm not carrying the gun you gave me."

Inside the courthouse the marble-tiled hallway was high-ceilinged and cool. On the walls were many oil paintings of judges and politicians, but the portrait of President Porfirio Diaz, lifetime president of the Republic, was bigger than any of them. Diaz looked very Indian in spite of

174

his gorgeous uniform and bushy Burnside mustache. The doors to the courtroom were already open and they went in.

In the front row of the spectators' section, Bannerman sat with the three gunmen. The only one he talked to was Cajun. The two Mexican gunslingers sat uneasily, turning their hat brims between their fingers. The windows were open the morning breeze brought in the smell of horses. In front of the judge's massive bench an elderly court clerk with a bald head, wearing a pince-nez, sat writing. After each paper was signed, he stamped it with a rubber stamp. Some of the papers had ribbons held in place by red seals. After a while an old man in a blue uniform without insignia of any kind brought in a pitcher of drinking water and a glass for the judge.

While Sundance waited, Jorge talked to the court clerk and had his name entered in a book. Jorge paid a fee and the clerk took it without looking up from his papers. "That pompous old bastard doesn't like me," Jorge said when he came back to his seat. "He doesn't think I have enough dignity."

The old man in the blue uniform let out a yell and they all stood up as the judge came in.

"That's not Mendoza," Jorge said in such a loud voice that the court clerk gave him a threatening look.

The judge, who was not Mendoza, was about fifty and so fat that he waddled instead of walked. He was dressed completely in light gray and the frock coat was tailored to hide his glutton's belly. He wore a pointed beard in the old French style and his coarse black hair was cut in military fashion. He had a cruel but weak mouth. Everything about him was self-important and threatening. After he settled his broad backside in the leather judge's chair, the court clerk announced him as "His Excellency, Justice Rosalio Colomo of the Provincial Court of the State of Sonora."

"What the hell is going on?" Jorge whispered to Sundance.

Judge Colomo had a loud, coarse voice

that carried to every corner of the big courtroom. "It is my sad duty to inform you that my distinguished colleague, Judge Esteban Muniz Mendoza, died in his home in Durango during the past week. I am saddened by his passing and can feel only humility as I prepare to take his place. Call the first case."

Judge Colomo didn't look sad and he didn't sound humble. The first case concerned a rancher who was suing another rancher for selling him a horse that he knew had worms. The judge lay back in his comfortable chair and pulled at his right earlobe while the clerk droned out the details of the case.

"It doesn't look good," Jorge whispered. "They put a horse with worms ahead of me."

"What do you know about him?" Sundance asked.

"Not much. And nothing to his credit. Colomo had the district south of Durango. He was a captain in the *rurales* before they made him a judge."

Jorge was still whispering when Judge

Colomo rapped furiously with his gavel. His lardy face was red and he continued to use the gavel long after the courtroom had been pounded into silence. "Stand up, Señor Calderon," he bellowed. "Stand up now and tell me if you intend to continue to hold a private conversation while this court is in session?"

Jorge stood up. "I beg your pardon, your excellency," he said.

"All right, then sit down and show some respect. We will continue with the case at hand now that the advocate from Morelos has agreed to pay attention."

The spectators laughed appreciately and Jorge's face grew tight with anger. Lucas Bannerman turned half-way around in his seat, but didn't smile. Then he turned back to face the judge. Sundance gripped Jorge's arm, forcing him to hold in his temper.

The case of the two ranchers didn't take long. After it came the case of an American who was charged with salting a gold mine in the lower Sierra. How to salt a gold mine had to be explained to Judge

Colomo. The accused had bought a worthless, worked-out mine, then loaded a 10–gauge shotgun with small nuggets and fired at the walls of the mine. The gold broke up and imbedded itself in the walls of the mine. Later the accused had brought some rich Englishmen to the mine. After inspecting the rich "deposits" of gold, they bought the mine for fifty thousand dollars.

Judge Colomo sent the American swindler to the island penal colony off the Sonoran coast for twenty years. And he seemed to enjoy doing it.

The cases dragged on all day. Even with the windows open, it grew hot in the courtroom. Judge Colomo drank a great deal of water and took two and a half hours for lunch and siesta. It was too hot to eat, so Sundance and Jorge went to a cantina and drank warm beer and fought off the horseflies that buzzed in from the street.

Sipping his beer, Jorge said, "What's the use of waiting around for Colomo to make more jokes. You know he's trying to wear me down by leaving my case till last. And maybe he won't even hear the case today. He can hold it over till next month, or the month after. Why don't we forget about going back in there?"

"A good reason to stay is Bannerman would like you to walk out. But you're right about Colomo. This is his first court day in Las Piedras, but he knew your name and that you came here from Morelos. That means he's been talking to Bannerman's friends or to Bannerman himself."

"Then I haven't a chance?"

"I'd have to say no. But you have to see this thing out. If you don't stay, you can't complain later. But, if Colomo rules against you, there will be some kind of record that he did. That's why you have to stay. You said if you lost in this court you would appeal to a higher court or go to the governor, even to President Diaz."

"Looks like that's what I'll have to do. I know I don't have a chance with Colomo, but it'll be interesting to see how he turns me down. He may be a judge, but he's a rotten lawyer."

They went back to court and had to wait an hour before Judge Colomo came out of his chambers, rubbing his eyes and yawning. It was then two-thirty in the afternoon and five other cases were called before the court clerk demanded that Jorge Amadeo Calderon step up to the bench. By then the judge had been to his chambers several times. Each time he returned to the courtroom he was more bleary eyed than when he left.

"Proceed," he told Jorge and settled back in his chair.

10

JORGE unfolded his brief and began to read from it. He said he was appearing as an "interested party" on behalf of certain United States citizens being held captive in the State of Sonora. He demanded that a court order be issued, requiring that said United States citizens be returned to American territory.

Feigning surprise, Judge Colomo sat forward in his chair, "Who are these United States citizens you speak of, Señor Calderon?"

"They are Indians," Jorge said, "abducted from the American territories of New Mexico and Arizona."

Judge Colomo smiled and got ready to deliver a joke. "Yes, Señor Calderon, the court is aware that New Mexico and Arizona are American territories. As you know, they used to be Mexican."

After the ripple of laughter washed away, Judge Colomo asked, "Since when have American Indians become American citizens? Is their legal status not 'ward of the government?'"

"For most of them it is," Jorge answered, "but in the American Southwest the situation is different. Many of the tribes there were Mexican citizens before the War of 1846 and they became United States after the cessation of the war. Their status—their special legal status—has not changed since then. Those living at the time became United States citizens—and so did their children. This is the law."

Jorge had brought his law books into court, but first he began to read from his brief. One of his books was entitled *Laws Relating to Treaties With the Republic of Mexico*.

Judge Colomo's jowly face darkened as Jorge read on. Up in the front row of seats Lucas Bannerman sat very still. It seemed to Sundance, watching from midway in the court, that for a moment

Judge Colomo looked directly at Bannerman, as if asking for instructions.

"The law is quite clear . . ." Jorge was saying. Judge Colomo held up his hand and cleared his throat. "Señor Calderon, what you are describing is an interesting sidelight in our history, and I shall certainly study it, but I am afraid this court has no jurisdiction."

The judge paused so Jorge could speak. "With your permission," Jorge said, "I must insist that this court has jurisdiction. The Indian captives I speak of are being held within the boundaries of this state. Therefore, this court—the Provincial Court of Sonora—has the power to hear this case."

Judge Colomo did not agree. "Where these captives—if indeed they exist—are being confined is not the concern of this court. What you are describing is a federal matter, perhaps a diplomatic one. I repeat, Señor Calderon, this court has no jurisdiction. Of course you are free to take your *case* into the federal courts. In time, I'm sure your *case* will be heard, however long it takes. First, however, I would like to make a few remarks before court is recessed until next month. In the law books there are dusty, all-but-forgotten laws that should never have been passed in the first place. Many were passed because of the passion of the times, or for political expediency. To invoke laws that have no true merit is, in my opinion, an attempt to use the law for a devious purpose. And, sir, you may take that statement any way you like. Case dismissed!"

Sundance had to dig his fingers into Jorge's arm to keep him from saying something that would give the crooked judge a chance to put him in jail. Once in jail, he would never come out again except in a coffin.

"Let's go," Sundance said, when the judge went into his chambers and the court clerk closed his big book with a bang. They got out before most of the crowd. Jorge was still trembling with anger when they got to the bottom of the courthouse steps.

"That fat pig, you heard what he said," Jorge raged. "That *puerco!* 'Devious purpose!' He said I was free to go into the federal courts. Who the hell is he to tell me what I can do! The federal courts mean Mexico City. It may take months, maybe as much as a year, before my case comes up. By then Bannerman may have run out of Indian slaves. So even if I win my case it won't make any difference to the Indians. Bannerman will have sold them far south of here. There is a big market for slaves in Yucatán. What the hell am I going to do?"

They had reached the other side of the plaza. "You are going to go ahead with it. I don't mean the federal courts but a direct appeal to the governor of the state and to President Diaz. Don't write to Washington until you have appealed to the governor and to Diaz. But let them know that's what you'll do if they turn you down."

"Blackmail the President?"

Sundance smiled. "Not blackmail. What you do is give the President all the information he needs, then let him decide. Diaz is very popular with American businessmen and politicians. The businessmen—the cattlemen, mine operators and railroad people—like him because he lets them plunder Mexico in return for millions in bribes. Diaz won't want any trouble with Washington just because of a few thousand Indian slaves."

Jorge said, "It can be dangerous to take such a strong line with Diaz. The secret police—the special branch of the *federales*—do anything he orders. Men disappear and are never heard of again."

Sundance was thinking of General Crook. "My friend, the general, has a few powerful friends in Washington. Also, Crook has a few good friends in Mexico City, mostly generals. If the word is passed along then you are not without influence, the *federales* won't harm you. I'd say you have to worry more about Bannerman than Diaz."

They got back to the street where Jorge lived and while the coffee was cooking they talked about what Jorge's next move should be. "I am thinking that an appeal to the governor of the state would be a waste of time," Jorge said. "I have written to him many times and have never received an answer. He lives in a fine house—a mansion—in Durango, which is many miles from here. He does not want to concern himself with what happens in a dusty little town like Las Piedras. I am told that he has never visited this town in all the twelve years he has been governor. I have decided I must be daring. I must go to Diaz. But getting to see him won't be easy. The Indian boy who was going to remake Mexico is now hidden away behind layers of politicians and soldiers. Men—lawyers, politicians, peasants—sit in his antechamber for weeks and months hoping to be granted an audience. That would be hell. You mentioned General Crook a moment ago. Will he really help?"

"Maybe," Sundance answered. "If I ask him he will—but I have to be sure I'm doing the right thing. Like I said, there are men in Washington—powerful enemies—who would like to destroy him. All he has to do is make one bad mistake and they'll be after him like wolves in winter. Crook can take up for you, Jorge, but it has to be done carefully. I won't ruin Crook's career, not for you, not for your Indians. Maybe that's wrong—but that's how it is."

"Do what you can," Jorge said.

"We have to watch ourselves from now on," Sundance said. "Bannerman is far from being a fool. He knows of my friendship with General Crook and what that can mean to you. When he had Silvestra tortured and killed, he probably thought that would put the fear of God into you as nothing else could. But today in court he saw he was wrong. I'm not sure we should stay in this place. Montoya and his men won't be any help if Bannerman's riders attack. Maybe they'll use dynamite."

"But where would we go, Sundance?"

"To a safer place." Sundance smiled as he took the coffee pot off the bed of glowing charcoal. "Wherever that may be. Meantime we have to think about getting you to Mexico City and Diaz."

"Ah, Mexico City," Jorge said. "It will be good to see it again."

Sure, Sundance was thinking, if you ever get there. Always at the back of his mind was the feeling that there was only one way to deal with Lucas Bannerman. Like George Crook, he believed in force —"preventive force," the general called it —when it looked as if nothing else would work. And yet he was forced by circumstances to give Jorge his chance. Though, by nature he cared for few people, he felt that he had a stake in this brave, drunken, often foolish Mexican. Jorge was a weak man who had forced himself to be brave, and to Sundance that meant a special kind of courage. There were men of courage who never thought about it—or very little—and they regarded death as inevitable and natural. Without pride, Sundance knew he was such a man. So, in a way, such men could be said to be men without a sense of courage. It was the weak men who were afraid to die and yet risked death willingly that Sundance admired. Jorge, the mad mescal drinker, was a very special man. Looking at Jorge, in his shabby black suit still smelling of benzene, and his scuffed boots, he felt a cold hatred for Lucas Bannerman. All his life he had fought against men, many of them as vicious as Bannerman, but he had been able to fight them in his own way, with nothing and no one to hamper him. It went against his savage nature, the Indian side of his nature, to hold back when everything he had ever learned told him what he should do. And yet . . .

"We better get started to Meseta to telegraph General Crook," Sundance said. "You might get to see Diaz without Crook, but it wouldn't be as easy."

Jorge looked impatient and showed it by scratching his head furiously, a habit of his when he was agitated. "Why Meseta? Meseta is north. If you want to come all the way to Mexico City with me, we can telegraph your general on the way. There's a telegraph office in Durango."

"Takes too long to get that far south,"

191

Sundance said. "By the time we reach Durango, he may have started down from the Border."

"Then you ride to Meseta and I'll head for Mexico City. I want to get this going."

"Not a chance," Sundance said, shaking his head. "If you start for the railroad at Durango on your own—you probably won't get there. First we'll ride to Meseta, then we'll wait for an answer from Crook. Then we'll make for Durango. You can go on from there by yourself, if that's what you want. That decision comes later. For now you stick with me. You've been in this fight a long time, so you can wait another four or five days. Don't argue about it, Jorge."

Jorge picked up a heavy law book and slammed it on the table, almost breaking the top. "You should have stayed in the army, Señor Sundance. You've got a natural fondness for giving people orders."

"Don't argue," Sundance repeated, but this time he grinned at the excitable Mexican. "We'll light out first thing in the morning, with your permission, of course. I don't like traveling in country I don't know that well after dark. Like I said, we'll have to watch ourselves. Bannerman may not try to get at you so soon after you brought this new case into court, but don't count on it. Don't ever count on what a man like Bannerman will do. So much the better if he thinks he has you licked. Get some sleep, Jorge. Diaz will think he's seeing a ghost if you walk in looking like the way you do now."

Jorge stretched out on the bed and Sundance turned down the lamp. After Jorge began to snore Sundance took the sawed-off and went down to the street to have a look. The moon was sailing across the sky and there was a dusty wind blowing in from the west. Washed by moonlight, the Sierra didn't look real, but high in the peaks the tigers were prowling. He looked up at the faint light coming from Jorge's quarters. Black beetles, drawn by the light, were ricocheting off the glass. The beetles fell to the street with broken wings, crunching under his feet. A huge brown rat ran across the street and disappeared into a doorway. Except for the sighing of the night wind, it was very quiet in the street.

Back upstairs Sundance bolted the door and stretched out on the floor, with his head on a rolled blanket and the shotgun beside him, where he could lay hands on it in a second. It was hot in the room with the window only open a few inches. Law books were stacked high on the sill as a protection against a stick of dynamite being thrown in from the street. Sundance grinned in the darkness. Jorge, cranky as ever, had been indignant about having his law books used as sandbags.

Now and then during the night Sundance woke, though not as an ordinary man might wake casually or nervously. It was something he had trained himself to do. Like his weapons, this special sense of time was part of his fighting man's equipment. But later there was no feeling of fatigue because he fell asleep immediately after he was satisfied that there was no danger.

By the time Jorge groaned himself awake at first light Sundance had coffee on the fire and meat in the pan.

"Sometimes I don't think you're human," Jorge said.

11

THERE were times, Sundance realized when Jorge could never leave well enough alone. This was one of them. They were crossing the plaza on their way to the north road and Police Chief Montoya was coming the other way on foot. The doors of the cathedral were open. People, many of them women, were going silently to early Mass. In the great tower of the centuries-old cathedral, the bell turned over and over, causing the morning air to shake with its vibrations.

Jorge was feeling cocky. "Look at the hypocrite Montoya on his way to church. If he enforced the law as well as he sang hymns there might be some law in this mangy town."

Jorge's voice was loud and Sundance told him to drop it. But instead of listening Jorge raised himself in his stirrups and called out, "*Policia*, can I depend on

196

you to protect my property while I'm away? I would hate to come back and find my property—my law books—burned."

Montoya, so closely shaved that there were several specks of blood on his chin, regarded Jorge with distant eyes. "Your property will be looked after, *abogado*." Then he walked away.

"Hypocrite!" Jorge said, turning his horse's head.

"Jorge," Sundance said patiently as they got to the other side of the dusty plaza, "you don't need any more enemies than you have now. You could be wrong about Montoya. He is a man caught between powerful forces. On one side there is this Colonel Almirante, on the other Bannerman and his politician friends. What do you want him to do?"

Jorge was scornful. "His job. Do his job or give it up."

The town of Meseta was about seventy miles away, and to get there they had to cross arid country, hills and plains that ran clear all the way north to the Arizona border. This was hard country where there were few rivers—and they all disappeared into the burning sands before they had gone very far. Ironwood grew plentifully on the plains.

They reached the mining town of Alamos after six hours in the saddle. They stopped there to water the horses and to drink very bad coffee in a ramshackle restaurant run by an old man with one arm and one eye. By then it was close to noon and the machinery at the two mines was silent as the men ate or slept in the shade. The old man who ran the restaurant was an American who said he had fought in the Juarez revolution. Sundance didn't believe him. The old man looked and sounded like a man who had lost his eye and his arm running from the law.

The old man had a round head on a long neck. His head was bald and shiny, his ears stuck out with batwings. His place was thick with flies and the smell of fried onions. "You hear about the Injun trouble?"

"What are you talking about?" Jorge

asked irritably. "You mean up on the border? The last I heard everything was quiet up that way."

The old man's single eye glistened with excitement. "Not up there, mister—down here. Last thing I hear, there's a band of renegade Apaches, Comanches and half-wild Comancheros raidin' and killin'."

Sundance couldn't drink the rest of the coffee. "Did you see any of this for yourself?"

"Nope—not me," the old man answered. "But I heard about it. A man come through here on his way south from Meseta."

"Had he seen it?" Jorge asked, putting a coin on the counter.

"I asked him that and he said no, but it's happenin'. I tell you it's happenin'. Soon it'll be as bad as up in Texas and Arizona. Course they'll have to get the army after them renegades. Goddamned red niggers!"

He saw the look on Sundance's face and turned away, mumbling an apology.

Later, on their way out of Alamos,

Jorge said, "What he said doesn't make sense. Indian trouble has always been far north of here. And even that's been quiet, if you can believe what you read in the papers."

Sundance was thinking. "It's been quiet," he said. "Even Geronimo has been behaving himself since General Crook got finished with him. And why would Apaches be joining up with Comanches and halfbreed Comancheros? I never heard of Comanches ever leaving Texas. I don't say it couldn't happen, but if it did the natural place for them to go if they headed south would be Chihuahua, not here. And Comancheros don't hook up with anybody for the good reason that just about everybody—white and Indian —hate their guts. Like you said, none of it makes sense."

Jorge looked at Sundance. "Are you thinking the same thing?"

"I'd say so," Sundance said. "Bannerman has a bunch of white men and Indians—their job is to start Indian trouble. If the people and the army get worked up enough, nobody's going to give a damn about Indian slaves. Fact is, they'll say the Indians ought to be slaves. I hate to say it, but your case won't be worth a damn if they succeed."

Jorge unstoppered one of his canteens and drank from it. His dark eyes were worried. "But who'd believe such a thing? You just said it didn't make sense."

"People won't be worrying about sense if enough killing gets done. No wonder Bannerman looked so pleased with himself yesterday. First off, he has this new tame judge jumping when he snaps his fingers. That takes care of the law in Sonora, least for now. Then he has this bunch of renegades out stirring up trouble. I'll bet the Apaches are real Apaches, stragglers from Geronimo's old band in the Manzana Mountains. The so-called Comanches and Comancheros would be Bannerman's whites painted up and dressed up."

"But why Comanches?"

"It figures. A lot of Texas people in Chihuahua and Sonora. They may not know much about Apaches—they do remember the Comanches. The Comancheros too. Anything to stir them up, is what Bannerman has in mind. It doesn't look so good."

While they were talking black clouds drifted across the sky and thunder rolled in the distance. A storm was blowing in from the east, coming over the Sierra, shrouding the highest peaks in darkness. They were in the hills now, still climbing up from the flats. After they crossed the highest point in the scrub-covered hills, they would begin the long descent to the plains again. Meseta was about thirty miles from where they were.

This was country where storms rolled in without warning. The thunder split the sky and for a short while everything— plain and gully and hills—were inundated. The ground underneath turned to mud. The rain was cold and the wind that blew was cold too. Then as swiftly as it came the storm would be gone and so would the water when the sun blazed down again.

Lightning flickered across the sky and the thunder roared like massed artillery. With his hat jammed down hard and his body braced against the pelting rain, Jorge yelled above the sound of the thunder, "There's a ranch down from the slope on the far side. If this keeps up maybe we'll stop for shelter."

Sundance remembered the place. He had passed it when he came south to Las Piedras. Black clouds like stained cotton were still coming from the far side of the Sierra. The cold rain came down in great sheets as the storm moved out toward the desert. Then the furnace would steam for only minutes and everything would be dry and hot again.

Drenched and cold they crossed the hills and then far below them, not far from the road, they saw the ranch, now almost invisible in the rain. Up on the Sierra it was getting light but where they were was still dark, as the storm passed over. The oily black clouds were moving fast and soon the storm would be spent.

Soon they reached the bottom of the

long descent from the crest of the low range of hills. Their horses' hoofs splashed through the churned-up mud of the road. Far away to the west, a rainbow lit up the countryside. The rain began to ease up, and before they got all the way down to the ranch, the sun came out.

"Looks like we won't bother with shelter after all," Jorge said. "We'll be dry as bone in fifteen minutes. No need to stop. Mother of God! What's that lying over there by the corral?"

Sundance had seen it moments before Jorge—a man with arrows sticking out of his back. There were two or three arrows. Now the sun was full up again and he saw the young woman sprawled not far from the front door of the low-slung adobe house. They rode in close and Jorge's face was white. The girl by the door wasn't more than fifteen and she was naked except for shreds of a bright-colored shirt-waist that remained about her neck. Blood thinned by the rain showed between her spread-apart legs, and she had been shot several times in the stomach. No blood came from the bullet holes in her stomach. Her face was a grimace of horror and her light brown hair, darkened by the rain, clung to her shoulders. Her eyes were open and her hands were clenched. Behind a water trough another girl, a few years older, maybe eighteen, lay sprawled in death. She lay face down in the mud, an arrow sticking out of her back. She had been raped too.

Sundance got down and snapped off the arrow shaft in the second girl's body. Jicarilla Apache. The door of the house was studded with arrows, Apache and South Texas Comanche. When Sundance went in, he found another dead girl of about twelve. Her head had been split and a tomahawk lay beside the body. He picked it up and inspected it.

"Junk—they sell these things to passengers at train stations in the Southwest," he said, his face tight with anger.

A long moaning cry came from the bedroom off the kitchen. Quickly Sundance drew his Colt and pushed open the door. A middle-aged man in a red shirt lay crouched against the wall under the window. His eyes were closed and he was trembling with fear.

"It's all right," Sundance said quietly. "They won't be back. Open your eyes now and tell us what happened. Stand up."

The man opened his eyes, but Sundance had to help him to his feet, then onto a chair. His eyes were glazed with shock. "All dead, everybody dead," he said in English. He sounded like he came from some part of Texas. "My whole family dead in a few minutes. After all the years—dead in a few minutes." He broke off and began to shake.

"See if you can find something to drink," Sundance told Jorge.

In the kitchen there was nothing, but Jorge went out to the front yard and found a bottle with a few swallows in it. He brought it back. Sundance uncorked it and held it to the man's mouth. It was then that he seemed to see Sundance for the first time. His eyes blazed with fury and his strong, freckled hands came up like claws.

"You rotten murdering Comanchero!" he screamed. He tried to get at Sundance's eyes with his thick fingernails. Sundance grabbed his wrists and forced them down by his sides. He had to shout to make the crazed man listen. "We're not with the raiders! Listen, do you understand what I'm telling you? We had nothing to do with it!"

Slowly the rancher relaxed and Sundance made him drink the rest of the whiskey. Now he sat up straighter in the chair, and the shake in his hands had gone. His voice was heavy, without any feeling in it.

"They came riding in from nowhere. No time to do anything. The old man out there dead is my father, the three girls are my daughters. My little girls . . ."

Sundance waited. Jorge's hands were clenched by his sides. Now and then he muttered something in Spanish.

"Please go on, sir," Sundance said.

"My woman is dead, seven years now,"

the rancher said. "Janey and me came down here to Sonora twenty years ago. The government deeded us a nice piece of land and we stayed on, built up this place. Good horse country. I tell you they came in so fast wasn't a thing I could do. Never had any Indian trouble in these parts and the *rurales* ran off the bandits pretty good. So no special need for guns. My old man was out by the corral, tried to run for the house, was arrowed down in his tracks. I was running for the house and I could hear my girls screaming. I didn't get to the house, not then. Something—a rifle butt probably—caught me in the back of the head. Not a real hard blow, more like a stunning blow. I was crawling into the house and I could hear them raping and killing my girls. They were yelling—in Spanish and some other Indian talk. The Apaches were yelling in Spanish, the rest of the savages in I don't know what. There were halfbreed Comancheros. One of the Comancheros raised his pistol to shoot me in the face, then this other halfbreed in a silver sombrero knocked the gun to one side. Then as quick as they came they were gone. Oh Jesus! Sweet Jesus Christ! My whole family wiped out!"

"Would you know any of them if you saw them again?" Jorge asked.

The rancher shook his head, then his eyes widened, "I'd know that silver-decorated sombrero. Silver stitching around the whole brim and crown. Never saw one like it. I never did get a good look at his face. Everything was going on at the same time."

Sundance helped the man to stand up. "I'm all right now," he said, sounding far from all right. "I've got to see to my people—what's there left to do but to bury them alongside Janey? Why didn't they kill me too? Then the whole family would rest together. What do they call you men, by the way?"

They all said their names. J. T. Flowers was the rancher's name, originally from the Big Bend country of Texas. "Thank you for the kind offer of your help," he said, "but it wouldn't

209

seem right—no offense—to let strangers see to my people. I'll bury them and read over them. That done, I can't say what I'll do."

Sundance said, "We're headed for Meseta. But we can stay awhile if you like."

Flowers shook his head. "What good would it to? I'm going to be alone anyhow. I guess you better tell the *rurales* captain what happened out here. Maybe he can track down these renegades. Doesn't make much difference—my family's gone away."

By the time they rode away J. T. Flowers was already sawing boards to make coffins for his murdered family. Soon the lonesome sound was lost in the vastness of the land and sky. Jorge remained silent for a long time, then he looked at Sundance with questions in his eyes.

"No doubt about it," Sundance said. "That was no real war party that attacked the ranch. They never would have killed three pretty girls and left the father alive.

They would have taken the girls and made them squaws. I've seen it too often to doubt it. They let the father live because they wanted him to tell his story. They murdered the girls to make it look as bad as it could be. The grandfather didn't count either way. It's Bannerman's men sure enough."

Jorge's voice was calm at last. "You know he has to die for this."

"I think he will at some point, but for now we'll go ahead and telegraph General Crook. You'll still travel to Mexico City to see Diaz. But yes, you're right. In the end, after all the talking is done, I don't see any other way of ending it except to kill Bannerman. It's one of those facts that can't be avoided. Even so, you give your law a fair try."

Jorge took off his hat and fanned some of the wetness out of it in the hot sunlight. It began to steam. "You think I'm wrong, don't you?" he said.

"It isn't that, old friend," Sundance said. "Like we talked about back in Las Piedras. How I feel doesn't count unless the law fails you. Bannerman has caused so much pain to so many poor people."

"What you're saying is, even if I win against him, you're still going to kill him?"

"It's something I keep thinking about."

Another two hours took them into the town of Meseta. The railroad that snaked across Chihuahua from El Paso and then into Sonora ended at Meseta. The town was joined to other towns in Northern Mexico and the Southwest. The town had the important air of a town that was going places. Nearby there were silver mines and big horse ranches. There were as many Americans in town as there were Mexicans. The telegraph office was at the El Paso & North Mexican Railroad depot at the north end of the main street. They could hear the clicking of the telegraph key as they came close to the open window. The air was thick with gray dust kicked up by horses and ore wagons. At the depot, Mexican infantrymen with carelessly slung rifles stood waiting to board a northbound train.

"What about the *rurales?*" Jorge asked.

"You do it while I send the message to Crook. Then we'll get something to eat and wait for an answer to come in. It's going to be a long message."

Sundance had to use two message blanks to finish all he wanted to write. Then he had to wait behind two drummers for ten minutes. He paid the telegrapher and walked around the depot until Jorge got back.

"What happened?" Sundance asked.

"The captain of *rurales* wrote it all down. He got all worked up when he heard how close it was to Meseta. He was yelling for his aide when I left. It'll be all over town in fifteen minutes."

After they ate two stringy steaks in a place kept by a Chinaman, they idled back to the depot and had to wait nearly two hours for the reply from Crook. It read:

HAVE ALREADY TELEGRAPHED OLD FRIEND WAR MINISTER FRANCISCO FIMBRES IN MEXICO CITY. WILL USE HIS

213

INFLUENCE WITH PRESIDENT TO OBTAIN INTERVIEW FOR CALDERON SOON AS POSSIBLE. HAVE ALSO TELEGRAPHED FIMBRES ABOUT COLONEL ALMIRANTE AT LAS PIEDRAS. SUGGESTED STRONG REPRIMAND OR DISMISSAL FROM ARMY. HOPE TO BE IN LAS PIEDRAS WITHIN WEEK. TELL CALDERON GOOD LUCK. CROOK.

While they were reading the message again, Sundance looked up to see a squat man in a silver sombrero watching them from inside the crowded waiting room of the depot. His face was brutal and flat, and he wore crossed gunbelts heavily looped with bullets. Like the hat, the twin gun-rig was decorated with fine silver wire, and his arms hung down straight from sloping shoulders. His arms were short so the crossed gunbelts were hitched up high. Sunlight glinted on the nickeled barrels of twin single-action .45 Colts. Sundance didn't take time to look at the killer's boots, but guessed they were as fancy as the rest of him.

Jorge hadn't seen him, so Sundance

said quietly, smiling while he said it, "The man with the silver sombrero is watching us from inside the depot. I don't see the rest of them, but they're probably around with the warpaint washed off. I have a hunch we're going to have company on the way back to Las Piedras."

"What about the *rurales?*"

"By this time they're out beating the bushes. We're going to have to do this by ourselves. Come on now. We're going to walk away from here and wait till it's close to dark. Then we'll move out for Las Piedras. They may try in town here, but I don't think so. It'll be on the road home. I don't think the gent in the silver hat knows I've spotted him."

Sundance and Jorge walked down to a bar called The Texas House. A smaller sign said: Welcome to the gentlemen of the Talcott Mining Company." Jorge had a bottle of cold *gaseosa*, a purple drink much favored all over Mexico by women and children. "This slop is enough to make a man start drinking again," Jorge said, sipping at his drink.

Sundance ordered a bottle of beer, and just sipped at it. Against the back wall of the saloon was a free lunch counter with soggy pickles and hot peppers. While they were talking, an Apache with his hair cut short, in white man's clothes, came in and stood in front of the lunch counter. He was wearing a loose canvas coat, a miner's coat, but Sundance spotted the slight bulge of the pistol belted underneath. After a while the "civilized" Apache came to the bar, bought a mug of beer and took his time about drinking it.

"I think I've spotted another of the raiders," Sundance said quietly. "He's right behind you, don't turn around."

Not much later the Apache finished his beer and went out. It was eight o'clock now. In another hour it would start to get dark. "What're we going to do?" Jorge wanted to know. They hadn't talked about it because the Apache had been there for so long.

Sundance smiled bitterly. "We're going

to trip them up when they start after us like the hammers of hell. But we'll have to find the right place, and even then it might not work. That hombre with the silver hat looks like he knows a few tricks."

"What's the trick?" Jorge asked, making a sour face as he drank what was left of the *gaseosa*.

"Just because you paid for it doesn't mean you have to drink it," Sundance said. "The trick is we put some distance between the raiders and us. It has to be just a little time into dusk. It can't be too light or too dark. If it's too light, they'll see the rope stretched across the road. If it's too dark, we won't be able to see to kill them."

Jorge nodded. "I am thinking of those lovely young girls they raped and murdered. If I can get close enough to some of them, I will use the knife. It will be a pleasure to emasculate them."

"Forget that, Jorge. Just do your best to kill them and that will do fine. You don't want to turn into a savage yourself."

He told Jorge how he had castrated and killed the men who had raped and murdered his Cheyenne mother and later his father. "I turned into a savage for awhile and I still think about it."

"I would think about it with much enjoyment. I would see it as a fond memory."

They used up the rest of the time talking about Crook's telegraph and what Jorge would do when he arrived in Mexico to see President Diaz. Jorge did not like Diaz and said so. Sundance had to warn him to be quiet.

"He betrayed the revolution, and the people are as poor as they were under the Spanish and the French."

Sundance said, "He's the man with the power—you don't have to love him. Come on, you patriot, it's time to leave."

12

ON the way out of town Sundance said, after thinking about it, "There's a good place about a mile this side of where the Flowers family was massacred. Plenty of ironwoods on both sides of the road. It all depends on how much we have to get set for them. We don't need much time, but we need some. What have you got there?"

Reaching down, Jorge had taken a thin-bladed knife with an ebony handle from his boot. The long blade glittered in the dying light. "You don't remember this knife? The night we went to get the American rifles at Vera Cruz and I had to kill the French sentry?"

"Put it away. I remember that knife. I'm surprised you still have it after all this time."

They were getting to the outskirts of the bustling town. Jorge slid the knife into his boot beside his leg. "It's a good knife. All these years it has been used for nothing but peeling apples."

"Then save it for that. Set your animal to moving a little faster. We have to time this right, or it won't go so good for us. Flowers said he thought there were at least six of them. That's enough to have to take on at one time. And there may be more than six."

They left the last of the town behind, traveling at a fair clip. It was about fifteen miles out to the Flowers ranch and the light was going fast. A few miles out Sundance looked back when he topped a hill. He saw them coming fast from about a mile back.

"All right," he said after they had gone another three miles, "put the boots to your horse. Don't fall behind or it'll all go wrong."

Touching the great stallion lightly with his moccasined feet, Sundance surged ahead. All the magnificent fighting horse needed was the touch of his heels, a soft word of command. As he rode Sundance glanced up at the sky. If they made it to the clumps of ironwoods, it would be very tight. The stallion put out more and more energy as Sundance raced ahead of Jorge. Finally he had to slow his horse to let Jorge catch up.

"The minute we jump down, run your horse ahead on the road. Use your hat, but don't yell. If the horse spooks and runs back the other way, it's going to be hell on us. When I pay out the rope, pick it up fast and wind it round a tree trunk. But let me tie my end first. If you reel in too much rope I'll be left with nothing. You hear?"

Jorge's gelding was lathered with sweat and he was gasping for breath himself. After the topped under rise in the road, they could see the lights of the Flowers ranch about two miles ahead. They got closer, with the raiders not so far behind them now, to the stand of trees. And, then for the first time, the raiders were close enough to open fire.

Sundance swung down from the saddle and landed on his feet while the stallion was still moving at a gallop. He had his rifle and the rope in one hand. As soon as his feet hit the sand at the side of the road, he ran to the closest ironwood and wound the rope around the slender trunk and made it fast with a hitch that wouldn't slip. Then he pitched the other end of rope over to Jorge, who grabbed it quickly and began to wind. When that was done, Sundance called out, "Move back—away from the road!"

The raiders came on, a mass of men without faces in the semidarkness. The last of the light glistened on a big sombrero with silver all over it. The man in the silver hat hit the rope first. He pitched over his horse's head and lay still in the road while the animal whinnied in terror and fell. Soon the road was a frenzy of wildly-plunging horses and cursing men. The rope broke, but it didn't make any difference now. Sundance opened fire a fraction of second before Jorge. He shot a man and shot him again when he tried to get up. Then he swung the Winchester and killed a rider who had managed to stay on his horse. From across the road Jorge was sending out a steady stream of rifle bullets, hosing the road with lead. Jorge killed another man. Sundance shot a man in the back who had broken loose without being hit and was running into the darkness. A man behind a dying horse shot back and got off three quick shots before Sundance and Jorge riddled him from both sides. Suddenly it was dark and there was no movement in the road.

Sundance walked out carefully and heard somebody crawling in the sand in the dark. He aimed at the sound and fired. The man grunted and died. "Stay where you are," Sundance ordered Jorge. "Our friend with the silver hat hasn't been heard from. I think he's still out cold." He was edging through the darkness when a pistol roared and flamed from nowhere. He felt a hammer blow on the side of his head, and even while he was falling, he heard the louder explosion of Jorge's rifle. Jorge yelled with wild rage and fired again. Then while Sundance felt the trickle of his own blood, he heard a scream that knifed through the sudden silence of the night—he knew what Jorge was doing.

Sundance untied his neckerchief and whistled for the stallion to come up. The big horse whinnied nervously at the smell of so much blood, so much fear. "Easy horse! Easy now!" Sundance said, unstoppering a canteen, soaking the neckerchief with water and holding it to the side of his head. The wound stung at first and it continued to throb after he wound the neckerchief tightly around his head. He walked over to where Jorge knelt beside the dead man with the knife in his hand. Jorge was sobbing.

Sundance clapped his friend on the shoulder. "You had to go and do it. Now you know what it's like. I told you to put that goddamned knife away."

Jorge wiped the bloody blade on the dead man's shirt and stood up. His voice was shrill and defiant. "He deserved it, the murdering animal. They all did."

Sundance's voice was flat and final. "Then go to it. They won't feel it, but if it makes you feel better. If you enjoy it . . ."

Jorge began to curse. "The hell with you!" Then he pitched the knife into the darkness.

"That was a dumb thing to do, throw away a good knife. But we won't try to look for it." Sundance pushed Jorge toward his horse who was coming back, still sweating badly. "Get hold of yourself. What you did is done and you can't undo it. If the thought of what you did makes you sick to your stomach, don't try to say you did it because of what he did to those girls. Face up to the savage— yes, dirty—side of your nature."

The front door of the Flowers house had swung open during the ambush. It was still open. "Let's get out of here," Sundance said. "Flowers can have what satisfaction there is in looking at these men in the morning."

As they passed the house, they could see the father of the murdered girls outlined in the doorway. There was no way he could see them. They started up and over the long slope that would take them back to Las Piedras.

"Ease up on that animal," Sundance ordered Jorge. "No need to hurry now. We want to arrive back in town with nice cooled-off mounts." There was a long silence. "How are you feeling?"

"Sick, like you said."

"You'll get over it."

"I used to peel apples with that knife and cut the ends off cigars before the doctor stopped me from smoking."

Sundance saw no reason to make such a fuss about it. "You'll have to buy another knife."

"I don't want to talk about it."

"What do you want to talk about, if anything?"

"Bannerman."

"You mean he won't like this. That's the idea for him not to like it. I figured it was just possble that he might back off after we did for all those men on the mesa. There was his chance to get out of the game with some chips. But, no, he went right ahead and got worse. I wonder how he's going to feel when the war minister goes after Colonel Almirante."

"You think your general has that much influence with Minister Fimbres?"

"As much as he needs. Crook and Fimbres have been good friends since the war minister was attached to the general's staff as a foreign observer during the Civil War. Colonel Almirante will think a rockslide fell on him."

They were in sight of the lights of Las Piedras. To the southwest of the town was the sprawl of Bannerman's *rancheria*, with its red-roofed building that sprawled over more than an acre. Men with rifles stood guard night and day among the lemon trees, behind the thick abode. Cajun, the deadly Louisiana gunman was there. So were the other pistoleros, and always the Apaches, cruelest fighters on earth. Yes, Sundance thought, a fortress.

"What about Bannerman's political friends?" Jorge asked. "What do you think will happen there?"

"Hard to say. We're a long way from Mexico City. Almirante has to obey the war minister's orders or get out. The politicians—a judge like Colomo—isn't under such control. No way to say what Bannerman will do. A man like that doesn't know how to bend, to cut his losses. As I see it, this *rancheria*, the mines and the rest of it, are what he thinks of as his last chance to build a private empire. Other Southerns managed to get over the war—never a stubborn, arrogant man like Bannerman. Nothing matters to him. I don't know that he even considers—thinks about—the destruction and terror he's brought about. No matter what happens, he'll go down fighting. Right or wrong, muleheaded pride is the word for it."

Next morning they were eating the breakfast they never got tired of, pan-fried steak and black coffee, when the rattle of many hoofs started down the narrow street. Sundance put down his cup and picked up the Greener 10–gauge and checked the double loads of buckshot.

Going to the window and moving the

stack of law books, Sundance said, "It could be Bannerman," but when he turned he smiled and put down the scattergun.

Jorge was always sour so early in the morning. "What the hell are you grinning at?"

Sundance said, "I guess Colonel Almirante is about to pay us a visit. See for yourself."

Jorge looked down at the colonel seated in a glistening black carriage pulled by four white horses. On all sides of the carriage were cavalrymen with tasseled sabers. Their horses were all black— black and glossy like the colonel's carriage. While they watched the driver got down from the seat and rushed to open the door for the colonel. There were two drivers; the other driver remained on the box with his arms folded, looking straight ahead.

"What the hell is going on?" Jorge asked.

"A demonstration of the power of the telegraph. Some man many hundreds of miles away taps a key and fat colonels run around looking scared."

"I don't believe it. The colonel is coming up the stairs. The fat swine is coming up my stairs."

"Then open the door."

"No, let him knock and ask to be allowed to enter."

"Damn it, Jorge, open the door. You've got to let the colonel save face. Not being any kind of Indian you wouldn't understand that, would you."

"That's right. Almirante is the son of a bitch who framed you into that guardhouse."

"It doesn't matter. Open the door. Don't act crazy even if you are—open the door."

Jorge shook his head and stuck out his jaw. "Absolutely not. Let him knock, then I'll decide."

Sundance went back and began to eat the rest of his fast-cooling steak. Colonel or no colonel, he was hungry.

Knuckles rapped on the door. "Señor Calderon, this is Colonel Almirante," a voice said. "I wish to speak with you. I bring greetings from a friend of a friend of Señor Sundance."

Jorge unbolted the door and, in spite of himself, Colonel Almirante looked with quickly hidden disdain at the cluttered little room, the unmade bed, the unwashed cooking utensils. The air was bad, Sundance knew. He didn't like it either. Jorge pointed to the only chair in the room and said the colonel should sit down. The colonel said he would prefer to stand.

"Once again, I bring you greetings, my own and those of the war minister, a man for whom I have the highest admiration and respect."

Jorge went on with his charade. "What can I do for you, Colonel? What do you need that brings you out so early in the day?"

The colonel's shaved and powdered jowls shook hastily. "Oh, nothing," he said. "It is I who wish to be of service to you."

Jorge nodded. "In what way, sir?"

The colonel spoke quickly. "It has come to my attention that you are planning a visit to our illustrious president, Porfirio Diaz. War Minister Fimbres has directed me to render you every service while you are in Las Piedras, but to also offer you an escort of my cavalrymen on your way to the train in Durango. If you wish to have a military escort during your visit to the capital, I am to provide that too."

"To the railroad will be enough," Jorge said coldly.

"Wait a minute," Sundance interrupted. "There's no reason why not. Since the colonel is being so kind . . ."

Colonel Almirante, considering his belly, did a fair imitation of a bow. "Thank you, Señor Sundance."

Jorge said, "I don't want soldiers following me around all the time I'm in Mexico City. I can see an escort to the train, but that's all."

"Whatever you say, Señor Calderon. And I hope when you meet the President, you will mention my name."

"I will if I happen to remember it," Jorge said. "And how is all this to be arranged?"

"At your discretion, Señor Calderon. When you are ready to leave for your visit, word will be sent to me at the fort. Then I will personally escort you to the railroad at Durango. Until then a squad of guards will be posted in the street downstairs."

Sundance cut in. "That will be fine, Colonel. I would say Señor Calderon will be leaving in a few days."

The colonel inclined his bullet head. "Will you be going with him, Señor Sundance?"

"I don't see why I have to do." Sundance made his point, so there would be no mistake. "I'm sure the War Minister has confidence in you."

"Yes, once on the train, Señor Calderon will have a comfortable ride to Mexico City. A fine seat, fine food, good wine."

"I think some sort of escort ought to go along with him, Colonel. Let me be blunt, if anything happened to Señor Calderon it would go hard with you. You understand, of course, that I am not making any kind of threat."

"No escort," Jorge protested.

"If you don't accept a military escort, I'm walking out on you. After that, you fight this fight any way you want. Just don't count on me to help you. I'll be up in the Sierra hunting *tigres*."

"All right, two men."

"No less than four," Sundance said. "What do you think, Colonel?"

The colonel had a film of sweat on his puffy face. "I think four should be enough. Four good men armed with rifles and sidearms. No one would dare attack Señor Calderon then. It's settled then, gentlemen."

The colonel turned toward the door and would have left if Jorge hadn't held up his hand.

"Yes, Señor Calderon?"

"We have much more to talk about, Colonel."

"Are you speaking of political matters?"

"If you want to call it that."

For once the colonel was firm about not discussing matters that were none of his business. "Those problems must be solved by the President himself. It would be improper of me to speak out before President Diaz has heard what you have to say. I think the War Minister will support me in this."

Jorge suddenly dropped all the formal language. "No matter what any son of a bitch says, I'm going to free every Indian slave in Mexico. Goodday, Colonel, I'll let you know when I'm ready to travel."

The colonel went puffing down the stairs and Sundance said, "That was fine, Jorge. In the States when a man is a hoss's ass, they call him that. No other name fits some men so well. It fits you like new boots. Will you ever learn not to get on the wrong side of people who could help you?"

Jorge sat down and hacked at his cold steak. "No, I won't," he said. "In the years I've been in Las Piedras I never once met Almirante in the street that he didn't look the other way. So to hell with the fat sneak and his politeness. He's only polite because he's afraid of the War Minister."

Sundance yawned though he wasn't tired. It was just that listening to Jorge could be like pushing a round rock up a long hill using nothing but your nose. "I guess it doesn't matter," he said. "I know what I'm going to do after you leave. I'm going to wait for General Crook, then we're going to climb up in the Sierra and forget all about you. We're going to hunt and fish for our meals, then bring back some tiger heads for the general's lodge in Colorado. Anyway, it looks like you're out of the woods at last. So am I. You won't believe this, but I like the peaceful life when I can find it, amigo."

"You were going to lend me money for the new suit. I'm all out of money," Jorge said.

Sundance grinned. "Yes, a new suit, new hat, new shirts, decent-looking boots. Even a razor with an edge on it. How does all that suit you?"

"Very good. Maybe I'll meet your general when I get back from the capital. If he's still here."

"If we're still here you'll meet him. Only don't start jabbering at Three Stars —that's the Indian name for him—the way you jabber at me. Three Stars is short on temper and will tell a man exactly what he thinks of him."

Jorge looked indignant. "Are you telling me I say crazy things?"

"Yes, I am."

"Well, sir, I'm not afraid of this Three Stars."

"You ought to be. I am. Come on now and we'll get you togged out for the trip."

"*Dios!* It may finally be over. All these years, all the people who have died, and it may at last be at an end."

"It looks like it," Sundance said.

13

FINALLY it was time for Jorge to leave for Mexico City. They were up with the sun. Jorge was going over his legal papers. It was a bright, clear morning. The heat of the day hadn't begun yet. Taking a pot of coffee off the fire, Sundance said, "Leave those papers alone and eat your breakfast."

Jorge shook his head. He had parted his hair in the middle and slicked it down with water. "No, nothing to eat," he said. "Coffee will do. If I ate something it would sit on my stomach like lead. I'm nervous, I want this to go right with Diaz. If I start with the head man and fail with him—then I'm finished. You think I have a chance?"

"It looks better than it did. Diaz likes to think of himself as the father of all his people, Indian and white."

Jorge drank some coffee. Outside the

town was coming to life. "How do I look?" he asked, picking a piece of lint from the lapels of his new black sack suit.

"Like a lawyer," Sundance said. "You look fine. You want me to go along?" They had talked about that the night before. "I'm still ready to go if you want me."

"No need for that. I'll be safe enough with the soldiers. I already feel like a prisoner. No, you stay here and wait for General Crook. I will never forget what he has done." Jorge smiled. "No offense, old friend, but you have the look of a pistolero. If you came with me to Mexico City it might be said that I was hiring gunmen. You are known in many places."

Sundance smiled back at Jorge, now fingering his glazed white collar. "They might say that," he agreed. "All right, we won't go over it again. You go with your army escort and I'll stay here and wait for Three Stars. It will be good to see him after all these months."

Jorge looked at his great old turnip of a watch. He clicked the case shut and said, "It will soon be time to send the messenger to the fort."

"Just about," Sundance said. "How long do you think you'll be gone?" They had talked about that too, but Jorge still wasn't sure. "I would think a week, maybe a little more. It may take a day or two to get in to see Diaz. Will you be here when I get back?"

"More than likely. Anyway, close by. I'll go down and tell the guard."

While they waited for the escort from the fort Jorge paced the room in nervous strides. Sundance knew it was no use telling him to calm himself. Finally Jorge said, "It's funny. If you hadn't come to the Sierra to hunt *tigres* I would be dead and my cause would be lost."

"That's how chance works," Sundance said.

"If it takes longer than a week, you don't have to wait here for me," Jorge said. He smiled ruefully. "After all, I am under the protection of Colonel Almirante as well as the War Minister. Leave if you have to. You have your own cause to fight. When this is all over perhaps I can help you in the time I have left."

"We can all use help, Jorge."

"You know, the odd thing now is I don't mind dying so much. I'd rather stay, but if I'm successful I won't mind going so much. You ever think about dying, Sundance?"

"Not much but I'm ready for it. I'd be in the wrong line of work if I wasn't ready for it."

Colonel Almirante arrived with the four troopers. The sun was up now and the colonel was sweating. The four troopers carried Winchesters and had holstered Colts. They were all mestizos and looked very solemn. Colonel Almirante was in his carriage, but he got out when Sundance and Jorge came down to the street. He smelled of sweat and toilet water, and looked as if he would rather be somewhere else. Across the street a crowd of Mexicans had gathered to watch.

The colonel's driver took Jorge's battered leather grip and put it in the carriage. "I have taken food for the journey," Colonel Almirante said. "Also wine and whiskey. '

Jorge said, "Water will do for me."

The colonel raised his tufted black eyebrows. "Of course," he said. "Anything."

Jorge held out his hand. "Watch out for *tigres*," he said.

"You too."

The carriage rolled away in the harsh sunlight, and when it was out of sight Sundance took his gear and went back to the hotel. He saw Luis Montoya watching him from the front of the *calabozo*. Two of his men were with him; Montoya didn't nod or speak. Sundance went on. It was hot and quiet in the town except for the usual barking dogs.

In his room Sundance worked on his guns; there wasn't much else to do in Las Piedras. A dusty wind stirred the faded curtains on the window. The morning dragged on and then it was siesta time. The town was quiet now. Even the dogs were quiet. From where he sat by the window he could see the jagged ridges of the Sierra. There were oak forests on the lower slopes. Pine grew thickly at higher elevations. Once the high peaks and remote valleys had been the stronghold of the Apaches, from which they raided deep into Mexico. Now they were broken and scattered.

Sundance put his guns away and went to the livery stable to see to his horse. The big stallion whinnied when he saw him. Sundance scratched the great animal on the forehead. "Won't be long now, boy."

The rest of the day was just as quiet. When it got dark he lay on his bed in the dark, listening to the sounds of the town. Down the street somebody was playing a mandolin very badly. Jorge would be well on his way to the railroad by now. Sundance smiled when he thought of the meeting between Diaz and Jorge. Diaz had started out as a champion of the peons and the Indians. Now he ruled like an emperor. Sundance hoped Jorge didn't lose his temper and tell Diaz what he really thought of him. Anything was possible with Jorge, and yet for all his craziness he was a real man. He had stood against Bannerman when there was no one to help him. Yes, Sundance thought, a crazy man—but still very much of a man.

Next morning before the town was awake, Sundance saddled Eagle and rode into the lower slopes of the mountains. It was still cool and the air was clear, good to breathe after the smells of the town. He rode higher following an old trail. Soon he was up high enough to look down on the town. Beyond the town, miles to the west, the desert began. The desert ran off into the distance, then disappeared in a blue-gray haze. It was very still on the mountain, except when an alarmed bird squawked into the air. On about noon-time Sundance found a fast flowing stream and let the stallion drink. He saw a few bobcats but no tigers. Like the oldtime Apaches the *tigres* lived as far as they could get from civilization. When Three Stars arrived they would have to journey far into the mountains before the hunt began.

In the afternoon, Sundance turned his horse and started back for Las Piedras. It was after dark when he got there.

Four days after Jorge left, Sundance was walking across the plaza. Colonel Almirante's carriage turned into the plaza from the south road. The carriage was filmed with dust; so was the colonel. When the colonel saw Sundance he ordered his driver to stop. Dust was caked in the sweat on the colonel's face. He was tired but smiling. "Ah, Señor Sundance," he said. "Your friend is on his way. The journey to Durango was without incident. I escorted Señor Calderon on board the train, my men with him of course. It was a quiet journey but a hot one. I look forward to a glass of cold wine."

Sundance just nodded and the carriage went on in the direction of the fort. He didn't like the colonel, and didn't trust him, but figured he was nervous enough to be careful, or at least stay neutral if it ever came to one final showdown with Bannerman. There was still no certainty that it wouldn't come to that.

A few hours later Sundance was eating a steak in the cantina when Lieutenant Novela, the British-looking Mexican, came in. He was by himself; his face was pale and drawn. Sundance looked up at him without saying anything—he already knew what it was.

Novela said, "You see my revolver is holstered. I do not want any trouble with you, Señor Sundance. The other trouble we had, I was just following orders. So no trouble—agreed?"

"All right," Sundance said. "So he's dead, is that it?"

Novela took a deep breath. "Yes. They stopped the train—some were already on board—and took him off. They disarmed the soldiers and tied them up. They took him off so he must be dead."

Probably, Sundance thought without much feeling. This wasn't the time for feeling. "How many men?" he asked.

"The telegraph said more than ten.

They were masked, all of them. It happened about an hour after the train left Durango. A place called Cubero."

"Where's Colonel Almirante?" Sundance asked.

Novela said, "Gone, Señor Sundance. After the telegraph message came, he swore he had done his best to carry out the orders of the War Minister. Now he is frightened that the War Minister will have him shot or sent to the penal colony in the islands. He is equally frightened of you—so he is gone. I think north to the United States. I am temporarily in command. What are you going to do?"

"Find Jorge."

"Do you want men from the fort?"

"Jorge had men from the fort, and now he's gone. Now I'll tell you what I told the Chief of Police. Keep out of this. I'll find the men who did this and after I kill them I'll kill Bannerman. You can run and tell him that, if you like."

Novela said, "I have nothing to do with Bannerman. I am not like Almirante."

Sundance didn't finish the steak. "I

don't care what you're like. Stay away from me."

Lieutenant Novela made a stiff little bow. "If that is what you wish. I have no orders concerning you, but may I say that I am sorry your friend is dead?"

After Novela left Sundance saddled Eagle, filled extra canteens and left Las Piedras on the south road, heading for Durango. He kept riding long after it got dark. The road was a military road, and traveling was easy so far. There was no doubt in his mind that Jorge was dead, out there in the wild country south of Durango. It wasn't desert country, but it was bleak and forbidding, with few trails, and the railroad ran through it like a knife. Jorge, the poor crazy *hombre*, was out there and he was dead. Sundance knew, as he always had known, that Lucas Bannerman would never let it go —but there was no stopping Jorge. He had had his chance, and now it was gone, and so was he.

Sundance pushed Eagle hard until the moon clouded over after midnight. Then he made cold camp in a clearing beside the road. He watered the stallion and drank some water himself. After that he rolled himself in his blanket and slept until an hour before first light. By ten or eleven that day he was a good part of the way to Durango. He rested the stallion at noon, then pushed on again. A hot wind blew from the south. He passed a few peons, and they stared at him, wondering who he was.

It could all be a waste of time, he realized. The country south of Durango was scarred with grown over gullies and dry watercourses. A hundred bodies could be thrown there, left to rot, and the buzzards weren't the only scavangers. The stink of decomposing flesh would bring them quickly.

Sundance knew what he ought to do was ride back and kill Bannerman, and yet he had to find Jorge, what was left of him by this time. It was something he had to do. Someone had to stand over Jorge, had to bury him and mark the place. No one else would do it. That was the white side of his nature, and now he let it have its way. Anyway, Lucas Bannerman wouldn't run away. He would stay at his fine hacienda, behind his wall of guns, confident that he wouldn't die until he was rich and old and honored. So he would stay where he was, and he would keep, for the time being. In spite of his cold determination, Sundance knew that killing the ex-Confederate wasn't going to be easy. Bannerman had lived through the Civil War; they said he had been a brave if brutal commander. Bannerman knew how to stay alive; he was one of those men who fight for life with every vicious trick at their command. And then there was the Louisiana gunman they called Cajun. He had to be good or Bannerman would not have hired him as his personal bodyguard. So he would have to die too. Anyone who stood in front of Bannerman would die.

It was close to dark, after resting the stallion twice, that he rode into Durango. Lights were flickering on in the town when he saw it from the top of a rise a few miles out. The railroad depot was in the center of town. It was the northernmost point of the rails that went all the way to Mexico City, hundreds of miles away. From now on he would follow the rails until he came to Cubero.

That night he slept in a livery stable with the stallion, and in the morning he continued on his way. The railroad ran out straight from the town. The rails glittered in the sunshine. When he had gone a few miles a train pulled by a spanking new American locomotive came from the other direction. Impassive Mexican faces stared at him from the windows of the coaches. A child waved at him and he waved back. The train sped into the distance, leaving a trail of oily smoke, and then it was quiet again. A bright-colored lizard darted across the track in front of him. The wind from the south blew hotter, and out in front of him there was nothing but the shining rails.

Riding easily in the heat, he came to Cubero while it was still early in the morning. He saw the water tower before he was close enough to see the few shacks that clustered around it. It wasn't any kind of town, just a stop on the railroad. Looking at the fading whitewashed political slogans on the water tower, Sundance thought, so this is where it all came to an end for Jorge. This was where they had waited to put an end to the man who had defied them to the finish.

There was a tin-roofed depot that had never been painted, and when Sundance came close, two Mexicans came out and looked at him. One of them, the older man, said in Spanish that he was the stationmaster. Yes, he said, he had been present when the masked riders took the man from the train. There had been no shooting, and it was clear that they had planned it all with great care. It was an outrage, the stationmaster said. The masked riders had ridden off to the west. He turned to point. "That way," he said. "Was the abducted man a friend of yours?"

"You could say he was," Sundance said.

At first there were no tracks of any kind because the soil was sandy and the wind had blown them away. But then he came to a stretch of rocks and gravel kicked up and chipped by many hoofs. The tracks went west and continued to go that way. Now he was about five miles from the train stop. It was then that he saw the buzzards, black against the sky, kiting in, getting closer all the time to whatever it was. It could be just a dead animal, but once again he knew it was not.

During his life he had seen many forms of death. The death of Silvestra had been terrible—but Silvestra was not a friend. He rode closer. If the new sack suit had not been lying close by there would have been no way of knowing that it was Jorge. They had stripped him and impaled him on the spikes of a bayonet cactus. Then they must have smeared his body with honey or molasses because, even now, what was left of him was still crawling with the huge red ants of the desert. Ants ran in and out of the eaten-away eye sockets, and the mouth. Most of the flesh on the body was already eaten away. It must have taken him many hours to die.

The only way to get rid of the ants was to burn them off, and he piled up brush around the body and set it on fire. Then when the ants were gone he scooped a shallow grave in the sand with his hands. One by one, he collected rocks and covered the grave. At last it was done. He stood up and looked at the mound of rocks.

"You started something good, Jorge," he said almost in a whisper, "and now I'm going to finish it for you. You can depend on that as you could never depend on the law."

The stallion, moving restlessly close by, whinnied now and then. A quick movement of his hand brought the big horse to his side. "All right, boy, let's get on with it," he said. "There's a lot to be done."

The thing now was to make a plan— one that couldn't fail. He thought about that all the way back to Las Piedras.

What was clear to him was that Bannerman, by having Jorge killed, had thrown a challenge out to him. A bullet would have been enough, but Bannerman wanted him to know that men who opposed him were not about to die so easily. Bannerman knew he would go out and find the body; that he would find it with little trouble. What Bannerman was saying was—I did it. What are you going to do about it?

Not far from Las Piedras he saw a troop of cavalry coming from the fort. Lieutenant Novela was at the head of the column and he reined in quickly.

"Did you find him, your friend?" he asked. "I have orders to proceed to Cubero."

"I found him," Sundance said. "What was left after the ants got through. He's buried about five miles west of the train stop. Tracks go on past the grave. I didn't follow them."

Novela looked puzzled. "But why not?"

"Because I already know where they

lead. Anyway, they have too much of a start."

"But I must go there, just the same," Novela said. "I will be away for at least a week. Do you understand what I mean by that?"

Sundance knew the point Novela was making: he wouldn't get in the way.

"Perhaps more than a week," the lieutenant went on. "It is going to be a long search."

Sundance nodded as the column moved away. Now he was free to go after Bannerman without interference from the Mexican Army. He had a week to do it in. Why not? If he didn't do it in a week . . .

Late that night when it was hot and quiet, with the window shades pulled down, he took the big Remington rifle from its wool-lined case and looked at it. Then he put it back and went to sleep.

14

VERY early on what might well be the last day of his life, Sundance went to the livery stable and changed the water in his canteens. The town was still asleep as only a Mexican town can be in the hour before dawn. In the hayloft above the stables the stableman snored heavily. Sundance watered and grained the stallion, checked the supply of dried deermeat, and then his other gear, before he started back to the hotel. He had already seen to his weapons, all his weapons, but when he got back he inspected them again. Gray light showed from behind the high peaks of the Sierra; first light from the east always showed itself far up on the mountain. There was something about the high Sierra that fascinated him, as it has fascinated the Indians for centuries. For him, as for them, it wasn't just a range of mountains. The Indians had a special feeling for the great mountain that he understood completely. Yes, he thought, it would end in the Sierra. Up there it would end for him or for Bannerman, or both. No matter if it ended for him too. Now his only purpose was make sure that Bannerman did no more harm in the world. There was no sense of nobility or self-sacrifice in his decision. At long last, after all the talk, it was something that had to be done, and he was the only man there to do it. If there were other men to do it—do it with finality—he would have stepped aside for he had much other work ahead of him, and he wanted to live as long as he could. But when he thought about it, it was the same work after all.

The mountain was where he would make his stand. In open country he wouldn't have a chance, no matter how well or hard or cleverly he fought. The odds were too great for open country. Up on the mountain he would become the hunted, but that was his intention, his plan, the only plan he had. Loading huge

.50 caliber shells into his pockets, he knew the heavy, long-range rifle would be his only chance to get out of this alive. They said the big sporting rifle could reach out and knock men down like the hand of God. Well, he didn't know much about the hand of God, but he knew what the Remington could do. But there was no certainty in anything, even with the .50. It wasn't likely that anyone in Bannerman's party possessed such a rifle, but you never knew.

He waited until the cantina down the street opened, then he ate a big breakfast he didn't have much appetite for. It was just part of the preparation for the fight ahead. The day could be a long one, and there could be more than one day. It was eight o'clock when he got back to the hotel. The owner's son, Anselmo, the boy who guarded his weapons, was filling coal oil lamps. He smiled quickly when Sundance came in.

"I would like you to do something for me," Sundance said. "You don't have to if you don't want to, but I will tell you there is no danger in this for you."

The boy, who wanted to be a soldier instead of a hotel-keeper's son, replied in Spanish. "I do not care about danger. Tell me what you want."

Sundance asked the boy if he knew the gunman they called Cajun. "A tall, thin man, an American. He works for Bannerman."

The boy nodded. "A bad man, I can tell. Yes, I know him, know who he is."

"I want you to give him a message from me," Sundance said. "You will have to ride out to the Bannerman hacienda to do it. Tell him I will meet him here—alone —at noon. In the street, here at noon. That's all you have to say. You say in the plaza."

"I will tell him he is a coward if he does not come," the boy said fiercely.

"I will never speak to you again if you say that," Sundance said. "You will no longer be my friend, do you understand? Swear you will just deliver the message."

"All right, Señor Sundance." The boy was reluctant. "I swear."

Sundance gave the boy ten silver dollars and told him to get going. "Alone, at noon," he repeated. "In the plaza."

He had picked up the challenge and he knew Cajun wouldn't come alone. They would all come, and Bannerman would come too. Sundance was alone, and they were many, so they would all come. As he always did when there was no turning back, he felt a great calmness. He moved with the deliberation of a man who knew what he was doing. But it wasn't the insolent calm of the killer who pushed a fight for the sake, even the love, of killing. For Sundance it was the knowledge that there was no other way.

As he walked to the stable to get his horse, once again he saw Luis Montoya watching him from the door of the *calabozo*. He hoped the Chief of Police would remain neutral, because he did not want to kill him too.

He rode out of town to where the first climb to the mountain began. It was just after nine o'clock now, and if he had judged it right the boy would be close to the Bannerman ranch. It was a short ride to the boundary of the big ranch. The boy had left in a hurry. He climbed a long ridge, then got onto the old trail that wound up the steep side of the mountain. He had ridden this way days before and had already picked the place he would shoot from. At that time he had hoped it would not come to shooting, now it had.

When at last he was out of sight of anyone watching from below, he dismounted and spoke a few quiet words to the stallion. There was no need to tether the animal; he never spooked no matter how fierce the fighting grew. Carrying the Remington, Sundance edged back the way he had come, staying low all the time, and then in minutes he could see down into the town. From where he was the plaza was more than six hundred yards away. Still too far. A shot was possible even at that distance, but if he missed there wouldn't be a chance to get another one. It had to be closer.

On his belly, with the Remington cradled across his arms, he inched down through wiry grass. Now and then he stopped, then went on again. A centipede raised itself threateningly only inches from his face. A sting from the poisonous insect could throw him into convulsions, but he was too close to raise himself up without the risk of being seen. His mouth was dry but he managed to spit at the centipede and it skittered off into the dry grass. For a long moment he lay still with sweat running down his face. Then he began to crawl again.

A little more than five hundred yards was as close as he could get to the plaza, because now the grassy slope broke suddenly and dropped down about twenty feet. It would have to be here. Pushing the big rifle out between two small rocks, he sighted in on the center of the plaza, dusty and sun bright far below him, with people moving slowly in the heat or sitting in the shade in front of the stores and cantinas. The cathedral threw a long shadow to one side of the plaza. When he moved the sights into the shadow it wasn't so easy to see. He could see after his eyes became accustomed to the shadow of the cathedral, but it couldn't be done fast.

While he waited the town went about its business. He couldn't see the *calabozo* because that was on the street where the stable was. The street was narrow and the houses on the east side of it were higher than those on the other side. Smoke from cookfires went up straight from the chimneys of the houses, then broke into spirals, and faded away. It was hot and dry up on the slope and he sweated while he waited.

He hoped but didn't expect to see Bannerman walk or ride into the plaza with Cajun. Bannerman was too smart for that—not scared, but too smart. Because that wasn't how you stayed alive, not why you paid other men to take your risks for you. As he had told poor dead Jorge— and it seemed so long ago—it wasn't true that bad men were cowards and good men were brave. What a good man like Jorge didn't know was that bad men were so often recklessly brave. Whether they knew it or not, they longed for death, and put themselves in its way by doing the things they did. Yet they struggled to stay alive so they could risk death again and defy it again.

Sundance, watching the town, wondered how long he would have to wait. He knew that Cajun would come alone if he had too; he would probably prefer to come alone. A killer like Cajun would always be looking for a man who could beat him, or try to, or die trying. For killers it was the same thing or, if not the same, much the same. You killed or you got killed. With real killers there was nothing personal in either. Sundance—no killer—understood.

He guessed it was after ten o'clock when he saw the boy coming back to town on the southeast road. It had to be the boy, raising the cloud of dust he was. He could see the boy when he was a fair ways out, and then he couldn't see him because, up high though he was, the tall campanile of the cathedral blocked out the view when he got closer. In five minutes the boy galloped around the side of the cathedral, and Sundance could see him clearly now, bareback on his pony.

He watched while people resting or sleeping in the shade or moving across the sun-bright plaza stopped what they were doing and gaped after the boy as he raised dust spurring across the plaza, then out of sight again. Though the gawkers didn't lose interest at once, they did after a while. The plaza resumed its usual morning quiet.

Nothing disturbed the plaza very much. Why should it? It was scarred by musket balls and bullet holes. Hundreds of men had been shot against its adobe walls, and even the ugly cathedral itself had been damaged by cannon fire. The cathedral stood. Tyrants and liberators, not much difference between them, had marched or straggled past it with their armies of accepting Indians and their foreign mercenaries. Whether the tyrants or the liberators had lost or won, the life of Las Piedras had remained, as it had for centuries, and as it would again. It would remain the same after all who were there now were dead, and their descendants were dead, and when even the oldest man now alive was dead—his flesh dust and his bones dry as sticks.

Then he saw them coming from a long way out. A dust cloud raised by many men and horses on the southwest road. After a while the dust settled as they slowed down to a walk when they got closer to town. He waited and let them come, the Remington at the ready, the big shell ready to be fired.

Now they were out of sight, as the boy had been, shielded by the mass of the cathedral. Sundance smiled. They were coming early to the party, getting ready for when he walked into the plaza at noon. Bannerman was thinking that he would play fair as Bannerman himself had played fair with no one.

They would be dismounted about this time and, with their horses tied on the far side of the cathedral, closing in from both sides. Suddenly the plaza was empty except for a dog that ran about in the center of it. The cathedral doors closed with a boom that he could hear up on the hill. Las Piedras looked like a town emptied by a plague or a gold rush. Five minutes passed, and then ten. They would have taken up their positions by now, after coming through the alleys and side streets. Nothing stirred down there in the town, and even the dog had run away.

Sundance squinted up at the sun, now almost directly overhead. He put the sights of the rifle on the far side of the plaza, and waited. He knew it was time when he saw a man scrambling across the roof of a cantina. It wasn't Cajun so he didn't try for a shot. Cajun was a man to be reckoned with; the odds would get a little better when the skinny gunman was dead.

Cajun walked into the plaza, a tall dark figure outlined in the glare of the sun. He walked into the shadow of the cathedral, and Sundance held his fire. Cajun walked out of the shadow, but Sundance wouldn't try for a shot until the target had stopped moving. Two more ambushers were up on a roof; the others would be in alleys and doorways, behind wagons. After he killed Cajun he would shoot at the men on the roofs. One of the men looked like an Apache, and he would be the second to die.

Sundance moved the rifle as Cajun walked with his measured gunman's tread. Cajun had been through this many times, but this would be his last walk in the sun. Cajun stopped walking and turned his head slowly. Sundance could hear his voice. Cajun was saying something, but the words were lost in the distance. Sundance didn't have to hear the words—Cajun was telling him to come out and be killed. Cajun was still talking, yelling now, as Sundance raised the big rifle and put the sights exactly where he wanted them to be. A little lower to allow for the extra hundred yards. Now!

The rifle boomed and far below Cajun

was thrown back ten feet. The .50 caliber bullet struck him and lifted him and dropped him in the dust. Echoes from the shot were still rolling when Sundance swung the rifle and blew the Apache off the roof. The two other men scrambled for safety as Sundance loaded another shell. One of the men got off the roof without being killed. The other man got the bullet low in the back and he went off the roof like a man trying to fly. That was it, Sundance knew. Three down— and how many others to go?

It was time to head out. If he stayed he could pin them down for a while. Later they would fan out and come at him from both sides of the slope. Even then he could hold them, but sooner or later one or more of them would climb up high behind him. Bannerman would send his best marksman up behind him. After that he wouldn't have a chance.

Answering fire came from the town as he jumped to his feet and ran up the slope. The fire from the town was heavy, but the range was too great. He ran over the top of the slope, crashed through brush and called to his horse. The fire from the town continued, but it sounded far away now, as if it had nothing to do with him.

Protected by the first shoulder of the mountain, he mounted up. "Start climbing, boy," he told the stallion. The shooting began to die away except for an occasional shot. Then it stopped.

The trail climbed straight up until it crossed a split in a ridge. It had never been a wagonroad, just a narrow trail for mules and horses, and there were no signs of recent use. The Indians had been driven out of the Sierra, and the only men there now were gold prospectors and hunters, but they were mostly on the far side of the range, on the Chihuahua slopes.

The trail went downhill for about half a mile, then began to climb again, all the time snaking its way up and into the razorback ridges that ran away into the distance. Many miles away the great peaks jutted up against the harsh blue of the sky. As he traveled, the old trail began to crumble away. It branched off in several places; the main trail itself became faint. It was hot and Sundance stopped to drink. Then he went on again.

It wasn't time to make a stand against them. At the point he was now there was plenty of cover, but they would have cover too. He wondered how long it would be before they started up the mountain. Not long, he thought; Bannerman would want to finish this. Unless he had figured wrong, that was what Bannerman would decide. Sundance was satisfied: so far it had been a good day's work: three men dead, one of them Cajun.

Unless he was wrong, Bannerman would have to take command of his little army. Sundance wondered how many men Bannerman had. He guessed ten or twelve.

Now he was riding up through the start of an oak forest, and the trees, twisted and gray, almost like stone, looked as if they had been rooted on the side of the mountain for a thousand years. Under the trees the ground was spongy and the stallion's hoofs made hardly a sound. It was very quiet.

Sundance was looking for the stream he had watered the horse at about a week before. On the far side of the stream there was a long bare slope that climbed. . . up into a line of rocks. The stream was fast and deep, the rocks in it were jagged. At that point, the place he had stopped, there was only one way across the stream, which came tumbling down from the heights in a white-frothing torrent.

He knew he could lie there at the top of the slope and kill them as they came. That could last for a while, but then he would have to head out again. There was no position secure enough that it couldn't be taken from the rear. Even with a cliff at his back they could come at him with ropes.

Leading the stallion across the stream at the shallowest point, he guessed he had about an hour's start on them. First, they would continue to throw bullets at the first slope. That would go on until they decided he had gone. But they'd be cautious starting up from the town. They had seen what the .50 caliber could do, and had done, and so they wouldn't be any braver than they had to be. The Remington was a terrible weapon to go up against. It was the range that awed and frightened men who faced it. Some of Bannerman's men might even want to turn back, or quit, but Sundance knew he would drive them on with threats and bribes. They understood both, and so they would go on.

Without fear, Sundance knew what would happen to him if he fell into Bannerman's hands. His death would be at least as horrible as Silvestra's and Jorge's. If it were possible, Bannerman would make it worse. So he would save a bullet, and if there were no bullets he would use the knife.

Across the stream now, he led the stallion up the crumbling slope and through a gap in the rocks. There was a step in the side of the mountain, then it went up again. He lay on his belly with the Remington pushed out through the rocks in front of him. It was a good place, as good as he had come to since he killed Cajun. Below him the stream foamed over the sharp rocks, a natural defense that Bannerman's men would have to break through before they could attack him at the top of the slope.

He could shoot them as they came across the stream, or as they tried to get across it. If some of them got across they would still have the slope to climb. He laid the Winchester .44-40 beside the Remington. The .50 caliber was fine for distance shooting, but it loaded only one shell at a time. For fast firing at a bunch of men coming at him at one time, the Winchester was the right gun.

He lay very still in the sunshine and listened to a bird singing on a branch. The bird and the rushing water below were the only sounds. There was no breeze, and it was very still on the side of the mountain. About half a mile up the first growth of pine began, and the trees carpeted the whole side of the mountain, green and dense. The smell of the pines was heavy in the sunwashed air. An hour later he heard them coming.

At first the sounds were very faint, though he guessed they were close enough but still cautious. The bird stopped singing and flew away before he heard the first sounds down on the trail. It could be anything, the fall of a rotting branch or a dislodged rock rolling in the shale, and so he listened and waited. Then he heard the scrape of iron shod hoofs on rock and gravel, and after that the muted voices of men. They kept coming but stopped in the cover of the trees about a hundred yards from the stream. They were in deep shade so Sundance held his fire. He kept his head down and waited for them to make the first crossing. One thing was sure, they wouldn't all try it together. It was very quiet except for the sound of the rushing water.

Under the trees, some of them would be sweating, knowing what they might have to face in a few minutes. Sundance knew what it was like to go up against a hidden gun. You walked out into the open, or you ran, not knowing if the next moment would bring a bullet crashing through your skull. Through the skull wasn't so bad, they said. Sundance smiled. Men who said that had never taken a bullet anywhere. A bullet, was a bullet. It was funny, he thought, that some men have a fear of getting a bullet in certain parts of the body, and they didn't always have the cojones in mind. Sundance had known a man who was deathly afraid of being shot in the nose. It was something he could not explain, but it bothered him just the same.

They would be coming out in a moment. They had to cross the stream. It was either that or turn back. Bannerman would never do that as long as he had men to do his bidding. Life was cheap to Bannerman but, like all such men, he held his own life very dear. Sundance knew that some of Bannerman's bravos were arguing that they ought to look for another crossing, upstream or down. That wouldn't sit well with the ex-Confederate brigadier. And it was always possible that Bannerman wasn't even there . . .

15

SUNDANCE knew Bannerman was there when two men left the shadows and ran toward the stream. The others stayed where they were, in good cover. From where he was Sundance could have killed the two men with two shots before they even got close to the stream. But to kill just two men wasn't what he had planned. Bannerman was using the army rule book: send out some men. If they aren't killed, then send out some more. After that, attack with the main force—maybe.

Sundance was taking a chance but he had to let them get across the stream. The two men, both Mexicans, looked up the slope before they went down into the stream, holding their rifles above their heads. Both were short men and the water came up to their chests.

Sundance lay back, showing only the

279

muzzle of the Winchester. He had rubbed the barrel with dirt to keep it from glinting in the sun. He knew he was cutting it very short, letting them get across with no certainty that Bannerman would send out any others. He had to decide how far he was going to play this hand. He watched while the two Mexicans climbed out of the water, then turned and waved back at the men in the trees.

Two more men ran out and Sundance let them get close to the edge of the stream before he opened fire. It had to be done fast because the main party opened up as soon as he fired the first shot. Sundance's first bullet slammed into the chest of the Mexican to the left, then he swung the Winchester and knocked the other Mexican back into the water. The current began to carry him away. One of the men on the other side of the stream tried to duck back the way he had come. Sundance got him next, knocking him down with two bullets in the back. The other man was firing up the slope, but making no attempt to run. Bullets sang around Sundance's head as he took steady aim and killed the man at the foot of the slope. Then he ducked down while they kept on firing from the cover of the trees. Lead spattered against rock as the firing went on and on. The firing was so furious that he knew Bannerman was trying to send other men across under the cover of the storm of lead. He rolled away from where he was and tried to find another opening in the line of rocks, but they were laying down rifle bullets from one end to the other. He had to roll right to the end of the rocks and away from them before he had a chance to fire without being killed. Now he was in tall dry grass but still no more than ten feet from where the lead was flying. He raised up and they were coming across all right, three of them. He got off three shots, killing one and wounding another, before the main force moved their sights and started blasting again. He knew he had to get out fast. If he didn't he was dead. He couldn't hold them here.

They had plenty of ammunition and were using it as fast as they could. He ran back to the stallion. The step-back in the side of the long slope to the pines kept him from being seen. So they kept on firing even after he was leading the stallion away. He had been wrong in his guess at Bannerman's strength: he must have started out with at least twenty men. Even with five dead and one wounded, he had all the men he needed. And in a minute they would be able to see him when he started up the slope to the first growth of pine. After that they would cut loose with everything they had. The range was fairly long and the elevation would make for difficult shooting, but if they got off enough bullets he might catch one or two.

"Move, boy!" Sundance said, and then man and horse were out in the open, running hard. For seconds nothing happened, then there was a chorus of wild yelling, and the rifles below opened up again. Bullets splintered the shale on the slope as Sundance ran behind his horse.

Bullets followed them all the way to the top, but they got there without being hit. They plunged into the cover of the thickly growing pine trees. Sundance said, "Go on, boy! Keep moving!"

He led the stallion up through the pines. Behind and below him the firing had stopped, and he knew they were coming across the stream. It was getting closer than he had expected. Bannerman's extra strength was making the difference. He would have to cut it down before they boxed him in somewhere, because with enough men Bannerman could just wait and wear him down. And now, for the first time, he wondered if he was going to get Bannerman after all. All he needed was one clear shot with the Remington, but Bannerman was too smart for that. He would hang back and tell his gunmen what to do. There was nothing to do but go on and keep figuring.

There was another deep shelf in the side of the mountain, and pines covered all of it. As far as he could see there was no break in the trees. There would be a break as he climbed higher and the tree-line gave out. Up past the timberline there would be nothing but rock and brush. In places the cover would be bad, but that was better than being caught in the pine forest where they could come at him from all sides. The pines grew too closely for riding, and the going was slow for a long time. By this time Bannerman and his men would be into the start of the pines. They would be more confident now, after having driven him back from the stream, but they would still be thinking of the Remington.

Sundance kept going for another thirty minutes until the mountain shelf started to climb up toward the timberline. The light was stronger as the trees thinned out and fell away behind him. He had to find his way through a huge scatter of rocks before he was out of the trees. The mountain loomed over him. No matter how high you climbed, there would be a step-back, and then it would surge upward again.

Out of the trees, he was in another

country: bare, bleak, dry, and cold. He knew he was up about four thousand feet. He climbed until he reached a sort of plateau that ran back for miles until the climb began again. It was a plateau split by ravines and impassable in places because of great upthrusts of rock. There was wind here, and at night it would be cold. On the plateau there would be no water; nothing grew there. As he started across it he knew there would be no place to defend here. He would have to get to the other side of the rock wasteland to look for a place. Before long Bannerman and his killers would be out of the pines, pressing hard on his trail. He could delay them a little with the Remington, but that wouldn't work too well up on the flat. They could spread out wide, keeping plenty of distance between them. While he was shooting at one point in their line of attack, the rest of the line would keep moving in. It wouldn't be long before some of them were behind him.

It was getting dark and he still wasn't off the plateau. It had started at noon and it was now nine o'clock. The wind on the plateau was blowing hard and cold. In the west the sky was glowing like fire; there was still some light, but it would be gone in minutes.

The last light of the sun went out as if it had been snuffed, and suddenly the plateau was cold and dark. The darkness gave him some advantage for a while, then a cold moon flooded the plateau in light that would allow Bannerman to travel as easily as during the day. Sundance guessed it was about another five miles to the end of the plateau. If he could get there, he might still have a chance.

It took him almost two hours to get there, because most of the distance was taken up by rock splits and fissures. He led the stallion over the bad places, mounting up when there was a stretch of level ground. But it was mostly all bad. Finally he was off the plateau. The moon began to fade and he knew there was still hope. Not much hope but some was all he needed. He kept on moving after all the light was gone, his moccasined feet finding footholds where a booted man would have had difficulty. Trusting him, the stallion followed over places that another animal would have balked at. He stopped to listen, but there were no sounds of pursuit. This was dangerous country where horse and animal could go tumbling into a fissure without warning. For now Bannerman was playing it safe, figuring to wait until morning to take up the chase again.

Sundance moved on for another hour. By then he was tired and so was the stallion. They had been going hard all day without rest, and the strain was beginning to tell. It was close to midnight when he decided to get some sleep. Up on the plateau it was bone dry from one end to the other. It was just as dry where he stopped to make cold camp. He spilled water in his hat and let the stallion drink. He drank a little himself after chewing on a mouthful of jerked deermeat. The meat had no taste, but it was food and a man could live on it as long as he had to.

Anyway, a man could go for a couple of weeks without food, and though his belly might growl with hunger, he would die of thirst long before he died of starvation. Sundance stoppered the canteen and pulled his blanket around him and sat with his back to a flat rock, the Winchester beside him. If they came in the night Eagle would hear them as soon as he did. But he didn't think they would come. They'd be rolled in their blankets by now, with horses tethered securely and guards posted all around. Bannerman wouldn't be taking any chances of a sneak attack in the dark. If there had been only five or six men, he might have tried it, but Bannerman's force was still too large for any kind of an attack. And then, too, it was possible that Bannerman had already split his force into two night camps and was waiting for him to attack one so the others could take him by surprise.

Despite the danger, he slept well. It was cold at that altitude, even with the blanket, but over the years be had trained himself to ignore heat or cold. White men found that almost impossible to do; with Indians it was a matter of necessity. If you were hungry all the time, as so many Indians were, you learned to ignore it, because there wasn't much else to do. It was the same with pain.

He was moving again two hours before dawn, still climbing up toward the peaks. The wind whistled down from the peaks and it was still very cold. Even during the day it would be cold. There had to be another place where he could wear them down, kill one or two of them, before he kept on climbing. His biggest concern was for water.

First light came early so high in the mountains. It came there long before it flooded the flatlands and the low country and the desert. But when it came there was no warmth.

Sundance moved on, leading the stallion, scanning the country ahead for a vantage point.

The sun was well up before he found it: a high rock the shape of a Dutch barn in the middle of a sandy depression about three hundred yards long. A fissure split the top of the rock and ran clear to the bottom. A man could crawl in from the other side and have a perfect V-shaped opening from which to fire. Heavy fire directed at the opening would eventually drive him out, but the depression was three hundred yards in length and the shooting wouldn't be all that accurate, especially if done fast. He rode around to the back of the rock and left the stallion in cover before he crawled through the huge rock and sighted on the country he had just crossed. So far there was no sign of them. But they'd come; Bannerman wouldn't turn back now. He knew if he turned back that Sundance would come after him again—and he would never know when. It could be a week, or a month, or at any time. Besides, by now Bannerman would be thinking that he had him beaten. He would follow him right over the top of the Sierra and down into Chihuahua, if that's what it took.

Sundance lay listening to the wind. Up

high it never seemed to stop. An hour later he saw them coming, but they were still too far out for shooting, even with the Remington. Even with his keen eyes, for the moment they were just men on horses, far out in the distance. He saw the flash of binoculars and kept his head well down. That would be Bannerman, glassing the country for an ambush.

It was the same as it had been at the stream: two men rode out in front of the others. They came ahead, walking their horses, rifles at the ready. Then when they thought they were still out of range, even of the Remington, they stopped and waited. Sundance waited for them to start moving again, but they stayed where they were. Bannerman was up to something, and Sundance didn't know what it was. It didn't matter. He wasn't going to hang around and find out.

It was going to be an almost impossible shot. One was all he would try, and maybe he was wasting time and a bullet he might need later. The range had to be at least six hundred yards. Seen across the sights of the rifle, the target looked no bigger than his finger. There was the wind to consider at a distance so great, but he went ahead with his calculations. He steadied the rifle until it was like a rock in his hands, and when there was nothing more to be done—he squeezed the trigger. The rifle butt jerked in fierce recoil, and far away a man died. Sundance didn't wait. He eased out of the crack in the rock and got away from there as fast as Eagle could carry him, and for a long time he was out of range and out of sight.

When there was no more protection from the big rock, he turned and looked back. They were crossing the depression but taking their time. Sundance rode on through country that continued to climb as far as the eye could see. Yet the highest peaks seemed far away, as if they could never be reached by any man. He made some time before watering the stallion and taking two swallows himself. After that the going was difficult because of the sliding shale and sand. It slid away under the stallion's hoofs. When it got worse he dismounted. A sand slide if it got started could bury them or send them rolling half dead all the way to the bottom. He turned and saw them coming, still a big party, and making fair time for men who had never been in this country before.

Sundance got himself and his horse over the top of the slope. When they got there he unlimbered the Remington again, and waited to see if he could get another shot. While he waited he saw the Bannerman force break in two. One part stayed where it was, the other rode out to the left. In spite of the Remington they were closing in on him. There would be no more surprises: by now they knew the greatest range of the rifle and to stay beyond it. The mountain was getting steeper now, and there wouldn't be anywhere else to climb. At a certain point it was sheer rock all the way up to the peaks. A man with ropes, nothing to carry and plenty of time might find his way up there. A hunted man carrying a rifle and leading a horse wouldn't get half a mile. It would have to be soon, Sundance knew. It looked like he had gambled and lost. Even so, he wasn't dead yet. What he would do was keep on fighting until the next to last bullet was gone. After that he would die.

Up where the rockface began he saw a cave sandwiched between the slope and the rockface. The opening was high and narrow and there was no telling how far back it went into the cliff. It was as good a place as any to end his life. At least here he could make a fight of it—all he wanted to do now. He scanned the country below him. They were still coming, now from different directions, keeping out of range of the .50. He knew it would take awhile to get up to the cave opening.

He knew he had to get up there fast. The way up to the cave was strewn with broken rock, but even so the only way to take it was head-on. If Eagle stumbled and fell before they got to the top, it could kill or cripple both of them. He thought of lying with broken legs under the dying horse while Bannerman's killers closed in. Then he rounded the stallion and rode back far enough to get a good start on the rocky hill. Eagle would have to get all the way up in one heart-bursting burst of energy. If the big animal faltered before he reached the top, there wouldn't be a chance of making it. It had to be up the hill and into the cave with no holding back, no stumbling or hesitation.

Bullets started to come at him from both sides. They hadn't got him lined up yet, but that would come soon if he didn't get out of there. He reached down and patted the stallion on the neck. "This is up to you, boy," Sundance said. "When I kick my heels you've got to go like you've never gone before."

"*Go!*" The stallion had about two hundred yards to get into full stride. The bullets were coming thicker now, and closer, as the stallion increased his speed, heading straight for the bottom of the hill. Then Eagle was going up urged on by Sundance as the Bannerman riders threw down heavy fire, yelling as they did so. When they were halfway up the hill, Sundance felt the big horse falter for an instant. Then with a great surge of energy they reached the top and were in the cave. In the semidarkness of the cave the stallion stood blowing wind and shivering. For the moment they were safe, because there was no horse in the Bannerman bunch that could take that hill, and there were few horses anywhere that could have done it. Men could climb it, but they couldn't do it fast.

Sundance emptied all the water that was left into his hat and let the stallion drink. Then he held the canteen high and a trickle of water ran into his mouth, a few drops, and that was the last of it. The cave had a narrow entrance, but it was roomy enough inside. It ran back about thirty feet and there was a bend in it where the stallion would be fairly safe even from ricochets. Yes, Sundance thought, I will have to save two bullets now, for he knew the stallion would serve no master but himself.

"Rest for awhile, boy," he said before taking his weapons to the mouth of the cave. Bannerman and his men were within range of the Remington, but they were staying low inside the near bank of a gully about three hundred yards out. Bannerman would have plenty of water, maybe a couple of mules loaded with nothing but canteens or Mexican water skins. Enough water to let them sit out there for weeks. And while they were waiting somebody could always go back for more. There was no hurry now, not for Bannerman.

Sundance lay on the rock floor of the cave and watched the gully. The wind stirred sand on the hill, and the sunlight was bright but cold. A hat came up on a stick, but Sundance didn't fire at it. The gully was deep and now smoke blew up out of it, driven by the wind. They were cooking coffee, maybe heating up brown beans with salt pork. Out there nothing showed but the smoke from the cookfire.

Then a rifle cracked and a bullet spanged off the side of the cave mouth. The shot came from the left, but by the time he swung the Remington there was nothing to shoot at. Another rifle opened fire from the center of the long gully, just two shots, and then nothing for a few minutes. After that they didn't fire more than one shot at a time, and it never came from the same place. It was a pretty good tactic, he thought. The Remington was a heavy rifle and couldn't be moved about as handily as a Winchester. There was no snap shooting with a Remington; it was a rifle for steady deliberate aim. Even so, he'd get one of them no matter how tricky they were.

In a few minutes he did. He kept the Remington's sights on the eastern end of the gully. He kept the rifle aimed that way even when two shots came at him from other parts of the rim. A bullet hit the rock not far from his face and whined into the back of the cave. But he kept the rifle steady. A man moved up to fire and Sundance blew him off his feet with a bullet powered by 40 grains of powder. The firing stopped for a few minutes, then started again. Sundance tried for another shot, but now Bannerman was moving the men after every few shots. He put down the Remington and started using the Winchester, but didn't hit anything. It was a stand-off that could end only one way.

Sundance stopped firing and counted his ammunition. There was enough to turn back a direct attack on the hill. For that he would have to depend on the Winchester and the long-barreled Colt. After that he would use the great ash bow; from it he could loose steel-tipped arrows as fast as he could hose bullets from the Winchester. He knew an attack would come, but it wouldn't be soon. There was no need for any attack—Bannerman would know that better than anyone—and yet it would come. Bannerman wouldn't give a damn if everyone but himself got killed storming the hill. Gunslingers could be bought for fifty dollars a month from the Canadian border clear down to Guatemala. Bannerman would want to get back to his fine ranch. Jorge had said that Bannerman lived in style, entertained lavishly. He and his second wife, niece of the Archbishop of San Luis Potosi, went on frequent visits to Mexico City. Yes, Bannerman would want to get back, so there would be a direct attack when he became impatient enough.

Sundance didn't take the time to inspect the cave for water. At a lower elevation, and in country that wasn't so dry, a drip of water from high up could sometimes be found. Not here. There was no water anywhere except in the canteens of Bannerman's men.

The sun was going down, and he wondered if some of them would try to come after dark. There was no way to tell. A man or men coming up the hill couldn't do it without making some noise, but most of that would be covered by the ever-present wind. The mouth of the cave and the country below it took on a red glow as the sun went down. Now was the time to get some sleep, Sundance decided. A night attack wouldn't come so soon. Probably it wouldn't. Sundance closed his eyes and was asleep.

He slept for little more than an hour, but it was the sleep of a man who had taught himself to sleep without fear or anxiety. The mountains had been blood red when he fell asleep. Now they were a ghostly white as the moon came up. From the gully came the glow of several fires. It was cold and the wind had an edge in it. He heard the stallion breathing in the darkness of the cave. It would soon be time to shoot the magnificent horse that had served him so well. The water was gone, and so was hope. If he let the great stallion live, they would take him and kill him with ropes and whips and cruelty, because they could never break his spirit. A bullet was better than that, but he would wait until daybreak.

He stayed awake, completely rested by the short sleep. He lay flat in the mouth of the cave, with the Winchester and the Colt loaded and ready. The bow and quiver were within reach. In the gully the fires continued to flicker, throwing shadows. He could see the smoke in the moonlight. Suddenly rifles opened up from two sides, and from the center of the gully itself. They had come out of both ends of the gully and were attacking that way. Lead spattered and whined. A fragment of lead sliced through the top of his ear, bringing a trickle of blood. There was no pain, just the blood. They were trying to bury him with lead, trying to drive him back into the cave. He fired and killed a running man, and then another, and still they kept coming. He swung the Winchester, looking for Bannerman. He shot another man instead. Now they were coming at the hill from both sides, while the shooters in the gully tried to keep him pinned down with heavy fire. The gun flashes were orange in the moonlight.

They were trying to come along the side of the hill, climbing up as high as they could. He had to risk being hit by the fire from the gully. He jumped to his feet and started shooting right and left. Two men were hit and went rolling down the hill in a tangle of arms and legs. A bullet made a hot furrow in the muscle of Sundance's right shoulder, but he kept firing until the firing pin dropped on an empty chamber. He pulled the Colt and emptied it, dropping two more men. Then he drove them back. They retreated on two sides, but didn't go back to the gully. There were two .44 shells for the Colt, about half a load for the Winchester, three shells for the Remington.

During the night they attacked again. He killed one man before they retreated. Now all the ammunition was gone except for the two bullets in the Colt. As the night wore on, they kept up a steady sniping that was supposed to set his nerves on edge. It didn't. The mouth of the cave was narrow and didn't offer much to shoot at from a range of three hundred yards. The firing went on as he waited for first light. He hated to kill the big stallion, but he forced himself not to think about it. It would be done when the time came to do it.

He picked up the ash bow. It was perfectly strung, a silent instrument of death. He nocked an arrow and tested it, then replaced it in the quiver. Everything was ready for what would be the last attack.

Cold morning light flooded the mountains. He got up but kept back from the mouth of the cave. He looked out at the beautiful, desolate world of the Sierra Madre. It would be there a million years after this day, after he was gone. It wasn't so hard to die once you knew it had to be done. Death could have claimed him so many times in the past, but he had gone on living on borrowed time. Now, at last, the debt was being called.

He took the Colt from its holster and walked to the back of the cave. Eagle whinnied and looked at him with reproachful eyes. "Life wasn't so bad, was it, boy?" he said. The Colt was already cocked. All he had to do was squeeze the trigger. He raised the pistol.

A sound at the mouth of the cave spun him around and he fired at a man who was bringing up a sawed-off shotgun to his waist. He fired fast and hit the man in the chest, but he didn't go down. The barrel of the sawed-off came up again.

Sundance fired the second bullet and the man fell backward from the cave mouth, the shotgun discharging both barrels in the air. The dead man, with a rope still looped around his middle, went rolling down the hill.

Sundance picked up the bow and quiver. They were coming in for the attack, what was left of them, maybe five or six. More than enough to finish him. The man with the shotgun had been lowered from the rockface above the cave. So they were up there too. While he waited Bannerman climbed out of the gully along with two men. Bannerman stood watching while his men moved in for the kill. Sundance counted six men running, driven forward by Bannerman's shouted commands.

The first of them reached the bottom of the hill. Sundance loosed an arrow that would have pinned the man to the ground if the ground hadn't been rock. He had to stand up and show himself to use the bow. They would hit him in a minute. They advanced at a dead run, firing as they came. Then a rifle cracked and a man died. The rifle—heavy caliber—boomed again. Another man dropped in his tracks. Sundance saw Bannerman wheel in surprise and bring up his rifle. The hidden rifleman fired again and Bannerman jumped down into the gully. Now the attackers, caught between the hidden rifleman and Sundance's deadly bow, turned and tried to go back the way they had come. Sundance killed one with a steel shaft in the spine. The rifleman killed another. And then Sundance saw George Crook rise up from behind a rock with a big English bolt-action sporting rifle in his hands. Crook shouldered the big bore hunter and dropped another slaver. Crook, wearing his famous canvas coat and flat crowned hat, waved at Sundance. Sundance waved back. Crook pointed toward the gully.

Still holding the bow, Sundance ran down the hill and made for the gully. It was long, narrow and snaked away for hundreds of feet on both sides. Up ahead he heard Bannerman scrambling over rocks, trying to make for the horses. He wheeled and fired at Sundance, then went around a bend in the gully and kept on running. Bannerman had reached the horses and was in the saddle when Sundance got around the bend. Bannerman raised the rifle and fired. Sundance didn't even think about the bullet or the rifle. Steadily, deliberately, he raised the bow and put an arrow through Bannerman's heart. The force was so great that he was knocked out of the saddle as though pulled by a rope. Sundance turned back to greet Crook. It was over.

It was night and they were sitting at a campfire on the lower slopes of the Sierra. Meat hissed in a skillet on the fire. Crook filled two tin cups with boiling-black coffee. Their horses and two pack mules grazed nearby. Crook lit a long black cigar with a burning brand and tossed it back into the fire before he lay back against a flat rock. "Ah, there's nothing like eating meat you shot yourself," he said. "One thing I can't stand—hunters who let good meat spoil."

Sundance wasn't thinking about food of any kind. He was thinking about chance. If that man hadn't come down the cliff on the rope when he did, at exactly the moment he did, the stallion would be dead now. If Crook hadn't arrived in Las Piedras a few hours after he shot Cajun . . . What was the use of thinking about it. Yet the thought persisted.

Crook knew what was in his mind. "I knew something was wrong when I arrived," he said. "I asked at the hotel where you were. The boy, Anselmo, wanted to help, but his father ran him off. I don't think he knew. Finally, the only one who spoke up was the Chief of Police, Montoya. He said he had figured out what you were doing. He said it was a crazy plan. Montoya was right. It was a crazy plan. But it worked."

"It didn't work, Three Stars," Sundance said. "Except for you my bones would be bleaching by now."

"Nonsense," Crook said. "But after

what Montoya told me I had to go up in the mountains and see if I could lend a hand. You and our late friends had a fair start on me, but I kept coming. It was an easy trail to follow." Crook smiled grimly. "I could have followed it just by looking for bodies. Bannerman wasn't the kind to bury his men. Lord, Jim, you killed an awful lot of men since you started out from that town. Wish I could have been along for those fights. Not a man you killed I wouldn't have been proud to kill myself. Slavers! After all the world's been through, Civil War, everything, we still have men trying to make slaves of other men. Well, I tell you, it won't happen again. That fat Indian crook, Diaz, won't dare let it happen again. Too bad your friend Calderon had to die. He must have been quite a feller."

"Yes," Sundance said, "quite a feller."

Crook looked at Sundance. "Well, Jim, we finally got to go on this hunt. You know, you damned halfbreed, I'd have taken it very personal if those slavers had killed you. Yes, sir, I would."

Sundance grinned. "Why is that, Three Stars?"

"A simple reason," General Crook said. "I'd have to break in a new hunting companion. I can't see a better reason than that. Can you?"

"I never argue with a general," Sundance said.

THE END

FARGO: MASSACRE RIVER
by John Benteen

Fargo spurred his horse to the edge of the road. The ambushers up ahead had now blocked the road. Fargo's convoy was a jumble, a perfect target for the insurgents' weapons!

SUNDANCE:
DEATH IN THE LAVA
by John Benteen

The land echoed with the thundering hoofs of Modoc ponies. In minutes they swooped down and captured the wagon train and its cargo of gold. But now the halfbreed they called Sundance was going after it, and he swore nothing would stand in his way.

GUNS OF FURY
by Ernest Haycox

Dane Starr, alias Dan Smith, wanted to close the door on his past and hang up his guns, but people wouldn't let him. Good men wanted him to settle their scores for them. Bad men thought they were faster and itched to prove it. Starr had to keep killing just to stay alive.

FARGO: PANAMA GOLD
by John Benteen
Cleve Buckner was recruiting an army of killers, gunmen and deserters from all over Central America. With foreign money behind him, Buckner was going to destroy the Panama Canal before it could be completed. Fargo's job was to stop Buckner—and to eliminate him once and for all!

FARGO: THE SHARPSHOOTERS
by John Benteen
The Canfield clan, thirty strong, were raising hell in Texas. One of them had shot a Texas Ranger, and the Rangers had to bring in the killer. Fargo was tough enough to hold his own against the whole clan.

SUNDANCE: OVERKILL
by John Benteen
Sundance's reputation as a fighting man had spread. There was no job too tough for the halfbreed to handle. So when a wealthy banker's daughter was kidnapped by the Cheyenne, he offered Sundance $10,000 to rescue the girl.

HELL RIDERS
by Steve Mensing

Wade Walker's kid brother, Duane, was locked up in the Silver City jail facing a rope at dawn. Wade was a ruthless outlaw, but he was smart, and he had vowed to have his brother out of jail before morning!

DESERT OF THE DAMNED
by Nelson Nye

The law was after him for the murder of a marshal—a murder he didn't commit. Breen was after him for revenge—and Breen wouldn't stop at anything . . . blackmail, a frameup . . . or murder.

DAY OF THE COMANCHEROS
by Steven C. Lawrence

Their very name struck terror into men's hearts—the Comancheros, a savage army of cutthroats who swept across Texas, leaving behind a bloodstained trail of robbery and murder.